Stacey and the Haunted Masquerade

Stacey and the Haunted Masquerade

Ann M. Martin

AN
APPLE
PAPERBACK

SCHOLASTIC INC.
New York Toronto London Auckland Sydney

No part of this publication may be reproduced in whole or in part, or stored in a retrieval system, or transmitted in any form or by any means, electronic, mechanical, photocopying, recording, or otherwise, without written permission of the publisher. For information regarding permission, write to Scholastic Inc., 555 Broadway, New York, NY 10012.

ISBN 0-590-22866-8

12 11 10 9 8 7 6 5 4 3 2 1   5 6 7 8 9/9 0/0

Printed in the U.S.A.   40

First Scholastic printing, October 1995

*The author gratefully acknowledges
Ellen Miles
for her help in
preparing this manuscript.*

Stacey and the Haunted Masquerade

CHAPTER 1

"Stacey?"

"Here!" I called out. Then I continued to draw suns, planets, stars, and hearts on the front cover of my social studies notebook. It was a bright, sunny fall morning, and I was sitting in creative doodling class, otherwise known as homeroom.

Homeroom. What a strange name. It's a room, all right, but it's nothing like home. Unless your home happens to have chalkboards, fluorescent lights, and seven rows of barely awake eighth-graders who are whispering, passing notes, brushing their hair, or scrambling to finish the last three questions of their math homework, while a teacher (Ms. Levine, in my case) tries to take attendance, keep some order, and make announcements.

I don't know about you, but, thankfully, my home isn't anything like that. For one thing,

1

my mom hardly ever takes attendance. (Just kidding.)

I mostly use homeroom as a time to gather myself together for the day. None of my good friends is in my homeroom, so I don't have anybody to whisper with or pass notes to. (Sheila McGregor and I used to pass notes back and forth, but we don't anymore, which is a long story I'll tell to you some other time.) I always take care of my hair and clothes before I leave the house in the morning, since both of those things are pretty important to me, so I'm never brushing my hair or checking my outfit in the classroom. And I never leave my math homework unfinished. English homework, maybe, but never math. I actually like math, and I'm good at it, so I usually breeze right through any assignments.

I always sit next to Sheila McGregor in homeroom. Why? Because my name is Stacey McGill, which means Sheila and I are alphabetically related. Like Sheila, I'm thirteen, and I go to SMS — Stoneybrook Middle School — which is in Stoneybrook, Connecticut. Unlike Sheila, and unlike most of my classmates, I did not grow up in Stoneybrook. I grew up in New York City, in Manhattan. (My parents are divorced, and my dad still lives in New York. Even though I chose to live in Stoneybrook with my mom, I still visit him there as often as I can.) And, not to be a snob about it, my urban roots do set me apart a little from the rest of the SMS student body. It's not that I'm better than them, it's just that I've seen more (including sad things, such as homeless people, and terrific things, such as the Caribbean Day parade) and done more (not too many kids in my class can say they've been to the opera, or to an exhibit of French avant-garde painters) than a lot of Connecticut kids my age.

I don't think I'm really all that different, though. Oh, sure, maybe I dress with a little more style and sophistication (I *love* to shop), and maybe my perm is a little wilder than most (my long blonde hair looks best when it's super curly), but basically I'm just your average, everyday teenager.

Except for one thing. I have diabetes. In case you don't know what that is, it's a lifelong disease, and a pretty serious one. My body doesn't make this stuff called insulin, which is necessary for processing sugars and carbohydrates. That means two things: one, I have to give myself insulin to make up for the fact that I don't produce it myself (I inject it, which isn't nearly as big a deal as you'd think), and two, I have to keep a very close eye on my blood sugar, which I do by testing my blood regularly and by being extremely careful about what I eat. I have to keep track of every bit of food I consume, every day. And sweets are pretty much out. When we first found out I had diabetes, my parents were incredibly over-protective, especially since I'm an only child. They've eased off a bit, because I've taken more and more responsibility for caring for myself. By now, it's almost routine. But even so, diabetes is a major part of my life.

It's only a part, though. I don't see myself as a sick person at all. I can do anything my friends can do (except pig out on chocolate bars), and I try never to let my diabetes bother me. And, while I'm definitely not glad I have diabetes, I think dealing with it has helped me grow up a bit faster than some of my class-mates.

Take Todd "Totally Immature" Long, for ex-ample. Half the time he still acts like a fifth-grader. That morning in homeroom, he was trying his hardest to drive Ms. Levine nuts by clicking his ballpoint pen about seventy zillion times a minute. Every time she looked up to see where the sound was coming from, he'd stop and give her this innocent smile. Then, when she looked down at her attendance sheet again, his smile would turn into a devilish grin and he'd start clicking again. Ms. Levine fi-nally decided to ignore the noise, which was the smartest thing for her to do.

I ignored him, too. I blocked out that irritating clicking noise by humming my current favorite song, "Sister Sally" (by the group Great Blue Whales) as I doodled on my notebook. By then I was drawing linked hearts with the caption S. M. + R. B. = LUV. My boyfriend's name is Robert Brewster, and I really do luv him. In fact, he's the most luvable guy I've ever met. I drew a string of hearts across the top of the back of my notebook, and I was trying to decide if I should keep going and cover the whole notebook with them when suddenly a storm of static erupted from the loudspeaker over the classroom door.

"Yow!" yelled Todd, clapping his hands over his ears.

"Why can't they fix that thing?" cried Sheila.

I wondered the same thing. I have never heard one announcement at SMS that didn't start with an earsplitting burst of static. It usually doesn't last long, though, and it didn't that morning. Soon, I could hear a voice through the noise. It was Mr. Kingbridge, our assistant principal. Mr. Kingbridge is okay, except for the fact that he has no fashion sense. I mean none. He wears the most ridiculous ties, the silliest jackets, and the ugliest shoes I've ever seen. At an awards night one year, he won the prize for worst dressed. I've thought of offering to be his fashion consultant, but I can't figure out how to do that without insulting him. After all, he's an adult. Supposedly, he should know how to dress himself by now.

Anyway, that morning the static took over the first part of his message, but we heard the tail end of it. "Go, Chargers!" he said enthusiastically. That meant he'd been talking about the SMS football team. I glanced at Sheila, who is a cheerleader. She was wearing a big "Go Chargers" button. She glanced back at me, and then looked away quickly. I don't think she has ever understood why I once turned down a chance to be on the cheerleading squad, or why Robert, who used to be on the basketball team, quit (he hated the special treatment athletes are given, and thought it was unfair). I think she *does* understand why I stopped hanging out with her and her friends, though.

Sometimes I don't understand why I ever wanted to be part of Sheila's group. I went through a very confusing time recently, when I thought I might be outgrowing my old friends, who belong to a club called the BSC (for Baby-sitters Club — more about that later). I'm ashamed to say that I treated those old friends horribly. But I'm happy to say that they eventually forgave me when I discovered that my "new" friends (Sheila's crowd) were not the kind of people I wanted to hang out with. I'm a member of the BSC again (I wasn't, for a while), and that makes me happy.

Anyway, back to Mr. Kingbridge. As usual, he was blabbing on and on, and nobody in the room was paying much attention to him. But then he said something that made us all sit up and listen.

Something about a dance.

A Halloween masquerade, to be exact. The first one to be held at SMS in twenty-eight years, according to Mr. Kingbridge. Immediately, even before I heard any of the details, I loved the idea. I mean, I'm way too old to be dressing up for Halloween, right? But part of me — the kid in me, I guess — misses the chance to be somebody else, just for a night. I began to think about costumes. I could be Cleopatra, and Robert could be Antony. Or we could be Bonnie and Clyde, or Jack Sprat and his wife. And if Robert weren't into dressing up, so what? I could be Marilyn Monroe or Wonder Woman. I could be anybody!

". . . and we'll need lots of volunteers to make sure this dance is a success," Mr. Kingbridge continued, his voice booming over the loudspeaker. "Let's erase those unpleasant memories of the past, and have a ball! Sign up as soon as you can to serve on the decorations committee, the refreshments committee, the tickets committee . . ."

Mr. Kingbridge droned on and on, but I tuned out. I was too busy thinking about costume ideas. I couldn't wait to see how my friends would dress up. This dance was going to be awesome!

Later, during lunch period, everybody was talking about the dance. I was sitting at a table with my best friend Claudia Kishi, who's in the BSC, and some other BSC friends: Kristy Thomas, Mary Anne Spier, and Abby Stevenson. Alan Gray was at our table, too, and so were Pete Black, our class president, and Logan Bruno, Mary Anne's boyfriend.

"The only thing I don't understand," Alan was saying, "is what Kingbridge meant by 'unpleasant memories.' "

Pete rolled his eyes. He reached into his pocket and pulled out a coin. "Here's a dime, Alan. Go buy yourself a clue."

"Huh?" Alan asked. "What are you saying?"

"I'm saying you're clueless," said Pete. "Think about it. The dance is scheduled for Friday night, and Halloween is on Saturday."

"So?" asked Alan, looking bewildered.

"So, Kingbridge has it all figured out. Friday

night is Mischief Night," explained Pete, "but if we're all busy with the dance, there won't be any mischief, so no 'unpleasant memories.' "

"Ohhh," said Alan, nodding. "That makes sense." For a second he looked disappointed. Then he smiled. "Oh, well. We're too old for shaving cream and toilet paper stunts, anyway. Right?"

The rest of us looked at each other in surprise, then burst out laughing. Alan Gray is the last person I would ever expect to hear say he's too old for anything. I can picture him pulling whoopee cushion tricks well into his nineties. But maybe he was turning over a new leaf.

"If you say so, Alan," I said, still giggling. "Anyway, the dance is going to be great. The only hard part will be deciding who — or what — to go as."

That was the beginning of a discussion about costumes that lasted for the rest of lunch period, and in fact, for the rest of the day. I wasn't the only one who was looking forward to dressing up. I guess there's a lot of kid in all of us.

CHAPTER 2

"Who ya gonna call?"

"GHOSTBUSTERS!"

Jessi led the chant, and we screamed out the response, then burst out laughing.

"I am already so sick of that movie!" exclaimed Kristy.

"It's on, like, five times a week," said Mal, "and I don't think my brothers and sisters are ever going to be sick of watching it. But I am. If I hear that theme song one more time, I just might — " She pretended to barf.

Ghostbusters had been playing on our local cable channel lately, and it was going to run through October. It's a fun movie, and I'll admit I've seen it more than a couple of times, but I knew just what Mallory meant. A month's worth was a bit much.

It was Wednesday afternoon, and my friends and I were gathered in Claudia's room, waiting for the BSC meeting to start. What's

10

the BSC? Well, maybe this is a good time for me to stop and explain. (Pay attention, now. There will be a quiz on this material!)

The BSC, or Baby-sitters Club, is a group of very different people who have one thing in common: we love taking care of kids. The idea for the BSC was a simple one. Parents can reach a bunch of experienced sitters by making just one phone call.

A simple idea, but a great one. The club has been a success almost from the beginning. At first, the BSC advertised with fliers and posters, but we hardly ever have to do that anymore. We have a long list of regular clients, and they know that they can reach us every Monday, Wednesday, and Friday, from five-thirty to six. There are seven members of the BSC, plus two associate members who help out when we're swamped, so parents are pretty much guaranteed a sitter when they call. And not just any sitter. BSC sitters are the best! Why? Because we care so much about our clients, and we go the extra mile to prove that.

For example, we keep complete records on our clients — not just names and addresses, but allergies, favorite foods, and other useful information. We also write up every job in our club notebook, so that all the members stay up-to-date on what's happening with our regular clients. And we aren't the kind of sitters who plop the kids in front of the TV while we gab on the phone. We love to play with our charges and keep them happy and occupied. Sometimes we even bring Kid-Kits with us. Kid-Kits are boxes we've filled with books and toys and games (mostly hand-me-downs, but they're new to the kids) and stickers and markers — all kinds of things. Our clients love them.

I missed the BSC a lot when I wasn't a part of it. I missed the meetings. I missed our clients. And, even though I had convinced myself that I had outgrown them, I missed my friends most of all.

The members of the club really make the BSC special. Somehow, the mix of personalities works. (For a while there, my personality didn't fit in, but I think that's in the past.) Sometimes when I look around Claudia's room during the meetings, I'm amazed that we get along so well when we're such different people.

Take Kristy Thomas, for example. She's the president of the BSC, and the one who came up with the idea for the club. That day, she was dressed (as usual) in jeans, a turtleneck, and running shoes, with a baseball cap plunked over her brown hair. She was sitting (as usual) in the director's chair at Claudia's desk, with a pencil stuck (as usual) over one ear. I watched Kristy eye Claudia's digital clock, and when it clicked to five-thirty, I mouthed the words along with her as she said (as usual): "I hereby call this meeting to order."

Kristy is *so* predictable.

But only in some ways. In other ways, she's totally unpredictable. Kristy's like a whirlwind, a tiny tornado (she's short for her age) that whips around, full of energy and motion. For example, besides running the BSC, Kristy coaches a softball team (called Kristy's Krushers) for kids who are not involved with Little League.

I've never met Kristy's father, because he ran out on her family quite a while ago. But I know her mom, and I can see that Kristy takes after her. Kristy's mom is one strong woman. After Mr. Thomas left, she raised four kids — Kristy and her three brothers (Sam and Charlie, who are fifteen and seventeen, and David Michael, who's seven) — on her own. That couldn't have been easy.

But things aren't so tough for Kristy and her family anymore. That's because Kristy's mom married this super-nice guy named Watson Brewer, who just happens to be a millionaire. Now Kristy and her mom and brothers live in his mansion, along with Kristy's grandmother, plus, every other month, Watson's kids from his first marriage (Karen and Andrew, who are seven and four); plus two-year-old Emily Michelle, a Vietnamese orphan whom Kristy's mom and Watson adopted together. Plus a whole menagerie of pets.

Kristy's home life is the opposite of mine. Sometimes I think I'd enjoy all the chaos and confusion of the Brewer/Thomas household, but mostly I prefer the nice quiet way my mom and I live. Kristy, on the other hand, thrives in her busy environment.

Kristy's best friend is Mary Anne Spier. Mary Anne is short, like Kristy, and also has brown hair. They both have brown eyes, too. But personality-wise, she and Kristy are like night and day. Mary Anne is quiet and sensitive and very neat. For instance, that day, as Kristy started the meeting, Mary Anne was bent over the club record book, updating her information on our schedules. (Mary Anne is the BSC's secretary, and she does a terrific job.) She erased something carefully, and then, printing precisely, wrote something else in its place.

Like mine, Mary Anne's home life is fairly quiet. She lives with her dad, her stepmom, and her kitten, Tigger. But Mary Anne's family has been through a lot of changes in recent years. First of all, Mary Anne grew up without a mom. Mrs. Spier died when Mary Anne was just a baby. Mr. Spier did a great job of raising Mary Anne on his own, although he did go overboard in the strictness department for a long time. He eased up a little bit when he remarried, though.

The woman he married happens to be the mother of Mary Anne's *other* best friend, Dawn Schafer. How that happened is kind of a wild story, but (deep breath!) here goes: Dawn's mom grew up in Stoneybrook and dated Mary Anne's dad when they were both in high school. But they didn't stay together. Instead, Dawn's mom went to college out in California, married a man named Jack Schafer, and had two kids, Dawn and her younger brother Jeff. Unfortunately, that marriage ended in a divorce, and Dawn's mom moved herself and her kids back to Stoneybrook. Dawn and Mary Anne met and became best friends (Dawn joined the BSC), found out their parents used to date, and brought them back together. (Whew!)

So now everybody's living happily ever after, right? Well, not exactly. First, Jeff didn't adjust to life in Stoneybrook, and he ended up moving back to California to live with his dad. Next, Dawn started missing her dad and Jeff, and ended up going out there for an extended visit. We thought that visit would get California out of her system, but no. It turned out that Dawn, who had always felt torn about where her "home" really was, decided that it was in California. So now she lives there full time, and Mary Anne is an only child again. It's been a turbulent time for Mary Anne, but she's handled it well. She has plenty of support, too. She and Kristy are closer than ever these days, and I know Mary Anne shares many of her feelings with her boyfriend, Logan.

Speaking of sharing, you'll never find a more generous person than Claudia Kishi, my best friend (and favorite shopping buddy) and the vice-president of the BSC. Claudia is Japanese-American and has long, shiny black hair, dark, almond-shaped eyes, and a complexion to die for. She's vice-president mainly because she has her own phone with a private line, so we can take BSC calls without tying up anybody else's phone. But, over time, Claudia seems to have decided that providing munchies for each meeting is part of the vice-presidential job description. I've never attended a BSC meeting where there wasn't food, and plenty of it.

Maybe calling it "food" is a stretch. I guess it depends on whether or not you consider Cheez Doodles and Snickers bars "food." Claudia sure does. She adores any kind of junk food, and always has tons of it on hand. (She knows I can't eat it, though, and she's very thoughtful about making sure she also has stuff I can eat, such as pretzels or fruit-juice-sweetened cookies.)

At that meeting, Claudia was rummaging through her bureau drawers, searching for a bag of Hershey's Miniatures she was sure she had hidden there. (Claudia has to hide her junk food, and also her beloved Nancy Drew mysteries. Her parents don't approve of either.) "Whoa!" she suddenly cried, interrupting Kristy, who was in the midst of asking if there was any new business. Kristy shot Claudia a Look, but Claudia ignored it. She pulled out a pair of purple, orange, and green paisley leggings. "I've been looking everywhere for these," she said.

"How could you miss them?" muttered Kristy.

Claudia grinned. "They are kind of loud, aren't they?" she said. "I love them." Claudia sees things a little differently than the rest of us. She's an artist, and color and texture and design mean everything to her. She has never received anything less than an A+ in art class. She can draw, paint, sculp, or create other kinds of art better than anyone else at SMS, but her grades in her other classes are more in the C range. Claudia's smart, but she just doesn't care too much about spelling, or algebra, or anything that doesn't have to do with art. Also, I think Claud figures her older sister Janine makes enough A's for both of them; Janine's a certified genius.

Claudia finally found the bag of chocolates and sat on the bed next to me, still clutching the leggings. She passed the chocolates to Mary Anne, who sat on her other side.

"Any other business?" Kristy asked.

There was none, but if it had been a Monday, I would have said it was dues day, and everybody would have groaned. You'd think I was asking for a pint of blood from each of them! Dues are no big deal. As treasurer of the club, I collect them every Monday and keep track of how much we have in the treasury. We use the money for things such as contributing to Claud's phone bill, paying Kristy's brother Charlie to drive her and Abby to meetings (which he's done ever since the Thomases moved across town to Watson's, which is about three miles away), and buying stickers and other things for our Kid-Kits. Once in a while, if there's enough extra money, we'll have a pizza party.

While I was out of the club, my job was taken over by Dawn. She was the BSC's alternate officer, which means that she could step in for any other officer who couldn't make it to a meeting. But now that Dawn's back in

California for good, we have a new alternate officer — and a new BSC member! Her name's Abby (short for Abigail) Stevenson, and she and her twin sister Anna and their mom (their dad died in a car accident when they were nine years old) recently moved into Kristy's neighborhood.

That day, Abby was perched on a stack of Claud's art books. She can't sit on the bed, because she's allergic to the feathers in Claudia's pillows, and she can't sit on the floor because she's allergic to dust. Abby seems to be allergic to just about everything. She's constantly sneezing, wheezing, and blowing her nose. She also has asthma, a disease that can be life-threatening. But she's learned to deal with it, just like I've learned to deal with my diabetes.

Her physical problems don't slow her down, though. Abby's a real dynamo. She even gives Kristy a run for her money. She's a natural athlete, with tons of energy for biking, soccer, or whatever. She's also addicted to fun. If nothing's happening, Abby makes something happen. We've always had a good time at BSC meetings, but it seems as though we laugh even more now that Abby's a member.

Abby and Anna are identical twins, but they're easy to tell apart because they dress differently and have different hairstyles. (Abby's hair is long, dark, and curly, while Anna's is short, dark and curly.) They both wear contacts most of the time and glasses occasionally. The twins are very different in other ways, too. Anna is a talented musician — violin is her instrument — and she's much more introverted than Abby. Despite their differences, though, Abby and Anna are very close and seem to have a special kind of connection.

Sitting on the floor near Abby that day were the two junior officers of the BSC, Mallory Pike and Jessi Ramsey. Unlike the rest of us, who are thirteen and in the eighth grade, Jessi and Mal are eleven and in the sixth. Being junior officers just means that they take lots of afternoon sitting jobs, since they aren't allowed to sit at night unless it's for their own families.

You remember I mentioned that for a while I felt as if I'd outgrown the BSC? Well, at the time, I had convinced myself that all the BSC members were babyish, and that Jessi and Mal were the most babyish. But you know what? They're actually both mature for their age. For example, Jessi, who's African-American and beautiful, with high cheekbones and long, long legs, is a serious ballet student who has been dedicated to dance for years. And Mal, who has red hair, freckles, glasses and braces ("a quadruple curse" as she says; she has no idea how pretty she is), is the oldest of eight

— count 'em, eight — kids, and she's been baby-sitting for ages. (Jessi's family is smaller, but she's a good sitter, too. She has a younger sister and a baby brother, and she's had lots of practice taking care of them.) Jessi and Mal both love to read, especially horse stories, and Mal wants to be a children's book author and illustrator when she's older.

And last but not least, we have two associate members: Logan Bruno (Mary Anne's boyfriend), and Shannon Kilbourne (a girl from Kristy's neighborhood, who goes to private school). (Associate members don't usually come to meetings. They just help out when we're overloaded with sitting jobs.)

Okay, ready for the quiz? Now that you've learned about every BSC member, this should be easy. Between calls at our meeting that day, the main topic of conversation was the Halloween dance and how to dress for it. All you have to do is try to guess which member was considering which costume to wear to the dance. (The answers will be revealed later on, for anyone who's still in the dark . . .)

1. Ballerina   A. Mallory
2. Lucy Ricardo (from   B. Mary Anne
   I Love Lucy)

3. Dorothy (from *The Wizard of Oz*)   C. Abby

4. Amelia Earhart   D. Claudia
5. Morticia Addams   E. Stacey
6. Cowgirl   F. Jessi
7. Giant Twinkie   G. Kristy

CHAPTER 3

Stacey McGill

There. I'd done it. I stepped back and looked at my name, which I had just written near the top of an almost blank sheet of paper. Then I smiled to myself and stuck the cap onto my purple felt tip pen.

I'm not much of a joiner. The BSC is an exception, a big exception. But, for the most part, I usually like to go my own way. That's why what I'd just done was a big step. I had been thinking about it ever since Mr. Kingbridge's announcement the day before. I hadn't talked to anybody else about it — not my friends, not my mom, not Robert, not anybody.

I looked back at the sheet of paper. "Decorations Committee," it read at the top. "Faculty Advisor, Mrs. Hall." The only other writing on the paper was my name, signed with a flourish. I was the first person to join.

It may not seem like a big deal, signing up

for a decorations committee. And it's not, really. But for me, it was a symbolic step. See, lately I've been feeling as if I need something new in my life. I mean, I'm thrilled to be part of the BSC again, don't get me wrong. But lately I've wanted to be more active at school.

I need the chance to prove myself, to have fun, to be involved. And the more I thought about it, the more I realized that working on the Halloween dance was the perfect opportunity.

It wasn't hard to figure out which committee to join. The tickets committee sounded totally boring, and being on the refreshments committee wouldn't be my thing either. The decorations committee would be fun, creative, and active, just what I was looking for.

I felt even better about my decision when I walked into school that morning and saw the sign-up sheets posted on the main bulletin board. The decorations committee definitely had the best faculty advisor. Claud has Mrs. Hall for English, and I hear she's pretty decent.

The first bell rang as I was standing there looking at the bulletin board. I needed to run for my locker if I was going to make it to homeroom on time. I skidded through the halls, feeling psyched. I couldn't wait to return at the end of the day and find out who else had signed up for the committee.

I thought about ideas for decorations during homeroom (Ms. Levine had to call my name three times before I finally answered) and through all my morning classes. I was full of creative plans. For example, I thought we should steer away from the typical orange-and-black color scheme. Why be traditional? Why not use, say, red and purple?

It's funny. Everybody (including me) is used to thinking of Claudia as the artist, the talented one. But I can be creative, too. It's true that I can't draw or paint the way she can, but I know I have a strong sense of style. During social studies class, I suddenly remembered something that happened when I was in sixth grade, when I lived in Manhattan. My mom had a friend who was an interior designer, and one day she saw my room. She was very impressed when she found out that I had done all my own decorating (at that time I was into an Art Deco look), and she told my mom that I had a "good eye," and that I could be a designer like her when I grew up.

Maybe being on the decorating committee was going to be the start of a whole new direction for me!

I was still thinking about decorating ideas when I walked into English class, my second-to-last class of the day. I took my seat and started to sketch out some plans for a fake gallows, which I thought would make a great set for the stage where the band would be playing. Mr. Fiske was taking attendance, so I didn't really need to pay attention yet. I was lost in my drawing when I felt somebody nudge me, and I turned just in time to see Amanda Martin toss a folded-up note onto my desk. I opened it and read it.

What do you think of the new guy?

New guy? I hadn't noticed any new guy. But when I glanced around, I spotted him immediately. He was sitting right next to me, and when I looked at him he gave me a big smile. He was cute (but not nearly as cute as Robert), with straight blond hair and brown eyes. He wore a blue denim shirt and khakis, and he was leaning his chair back on two legs, looking totally mellow. I was impressed. I doubt I ever appeared that relaxed when I was new at SMS.

I turned Amanda's note over and wrote on the other side.

Hunky! What's his name?

I tossed her the note just as Mr. Fiske was finishing up attendance. Amanda opened it, read it, looked at me, and shrugged. I looked back at the new boy, and he smiled at me again. This time, he even added a wink. I felt myself blushing.

Just then, Mr. Fiske put down his attendance book and sat on the corner of his desk. "People, may I have your attention?" he asked.

"I can tell you want attention just by looking at your tie," cracked Rick Chow, who was sitting in the front row. Everybody laughed, including Mr. Fiske. He's the kind of teacher you can joke with.

"Like it?" he asked, looking down at his tie. Mr. Fiske is known for his silly ties, and this one was no exception. It was bright yellow, and it was covered with red punctuation marks: exclamation points, question marks, commas, you name it. Just the thing for an English teacher.

"Very tasteful," called out the new boy. "Simple, yet elegant."

Everybody cracked up again.

"Why, thank you, Cary," said Mr. Fiske. "You may be new in town, but obviously you've already spotted the best-dressed teacher at SMS." He gave the new boy a little bow. "Class, I'd like you to welcome Cary Retlin. Cary just moved here from — " he checked a card on his desk " — Oak Hill,

Illinois. Welcome to SMS, Cary."

Cary smiled. "Thanks," he said. "This seems like a cool school." He was still leaning back in his chair.

"Cool enough," said Mr. Fiske. "Now, for today we're going to do a little free reading while I meet with each of you privately to go over last week's quiz. Cary, if you need a book there are plenty on the shelves over there." He waved toward the back of the room.

Free reading time in Mr. Fiske's class is generally an excuse to hang out. Some kids really do read, but most of us use the time to trade gossip or talk about what movies we saw over the weekend. Mr. Fiske doesn't mind too much, as long as he knows we keep up with our reading at home.

I pulled out my book, but I couldn't concentrate with everybody around me talking. I noticed that Cary was already engaged in a whispered discussion about sports with some of the guys. He seemed completely at ease, talking and laughing and cracking jokes.

Mr. Fiske called me up to his desk and reviewed my quiz with me. I'd done pretty well — I missed only two questions — so it didn't take long. As I returned to my seat, I saw that Cary was tipped back in his chair again. The kids around him were laughing as he read out loud in a funny voice from the book he'd chosen.

Suddenly, just as I passed by him, Cary's chair tipped too far over, and dumped him onto the floor. The room was silent for a second as the other kids stopped talking and laughing, out of surprise. I let out a loud giggle. I just couldn't help myself. Cary glanced up at me, and an odd expression crossed his face, an expression I couldn't quite read. Was he angry? Were his feelings hurt?

I stopped giggling and held out my hand to help him up. "Are you okay?" I asked.

"I'm fine," he said. By then he was grinning again. He turned to face the rest of the class. "And the judges are holding up their scorecards," he said, pretending to speak into a microphone. "Retlin is receiving some pretty high marks for that dive! Eight point six, eight point seven, eight point four, and — this is amazing! — nine point seven from the Canadian judge! Retlin is in first place!" Cary held his hands over his head and acknowledged pretend cheers from a pretend audience. "Thank you, thank you."

"Mr. Retlin," said Mr. Fiske, in a warning tone.

Cary sat down, but not before he'd given me another smile and a wink. I shook my head, as if to clear it. This guy was a real live wire. English class was definitely going to be more interesting from now on.

Later, after math class, I made a dash for the bulletin board. I couldn't wait to see who else had signed up for the decorating committee. As I moved closer to the sign-up sheets, I could see that a few names were listed after mine. I walked up to the board and started reading. "Rick Chow, Todd Long, Grace Blume — " So far, the list looked fine. My friends and I didn't used to like Grace much, but lately we've discovered that she can be okay. I peered closer at the last name on the list, which was written quickly and sloppily. And when I'd deciphered it, my heart sank. Cokie Mason. Great.

Cokie (who is Grace Blume's best friend) is probably my least favorite person at SMS. She's petty, small-minded, devious, and totally unscrupulous. (That's one of Mr. Fiske's vocabulary words. It means "without scruples." Cokie wouldn't know a scruple if it bit her.) I know that description makes her sound more like a soap opera character than an eighth-grade girl, but it's true. Cokie will stop at nothing to get what she wants, and the BSC has been "Cokified" more than once. Believe it or not, one time she even went so far as to try to steal Logan away from sweet, sensitive, wouldn't-hurt-a-fly Mary Anne. (I could have smacked her for that.)

I turned away from the bulletin board, trying to fight my disappointment. I had been looking forward to the first meeting of the decorating committee, but now I wasn't so eager. Still, I had to make the best of it, and not let Cokie ruin things for me. After all, why give her the satisfaction?

CHAPTER 4

Mal, your brothers and sisters *Saturday* are the best. I had a blast with them!

They loved you, too, Abby. In fact, they keep asking when you're coming back to play with them again.

Anytime. As long as they let me be chief ghostbuster, that is!

"Welcome! I am the Gatekeeper!"

"Nice to meet you, Gatekeeper," said Abby, shaking Nicky's hand. "Still looking for that Keymaster, are you?"

"How did you know?" asked Nicky, Mallory's eight-year-old brother. He dropped the deep voice he'd put on when he answered Abby's knock at the Pikes' front door. He'd been imitating a character from *Ghostbusters*.

"I'm a CPG," said Abby matter-of-factly.

"A what?" asked Nicky.

"A CPG," repeated Abby. "A Certified Public Ghostbuster. I'd show you my badge, but I left it at home."

Nicky's eyes grew round. Then he turned and ran toward the living room. "Hey, guys! Guys!" he shouted. "Guess what?"

Abby turned to Mal, who had answered the door along with Nicky, and grinned. Mal grinned back. "He's impressed," she said. "They just watched *Ghostbusters* — again. I can't believe they're not tired of it yet." Then she turned and called out, "Hey, everybody! Come say hi to Abby."

It was a rainy, gloomy Saturday afternoon, which meant that the Pike home was crammed with bored kids who had been stuck inside all morning. Abby and Mal were sitting while Mr. and Mrs. Pike went to a wedding.

Now, Abby had already met the Pikes, but just barely. That's why, Mal told us later, she was so impressed by the way Abby remembered all their names, plus something about each one of them.

"Hey, Jordan," she said, as one of Mal's ten-year-old brothers (there are three: they're identical triplets) barreled into the front hall. "How are the piano lessons going?"

"Okay, I guess," Jordan replied, just as the other two triplets came running in after him.

"Byron! Adam!" said Abby. "What's up?"

"We just spotted a ghost!" exclaimed Byron, who was armed with a plastic ray gun.

"A huge one!" Adam added, brandishing his own weapon, which looked suspiciously like an old vacuum-cleaner hose.

"Any ectoplasmic residue?" Abby asked, without missing a beat.

"Tons!" said Adam. "We were slimed in a big way." He grinned, as if being slimed were something to be happy about. Then he and the other two ran off, shouting something about telekinetic activity.

No sooner had they left than Vanessa showed up, with Margo and Claire in tow. "Hi, Vanessa," Abby said. "Written any new poems lately?"

"Lots," said Vanessa, who's nine and wants

to be a poet (she's already written volumes and volumes of verse). "Want to hear the one I'm working on today?" she asked. "It's called 'The Haunting of Pike House.' It's going to be an epic, but so far it's only three pages long. It starts off like this: 'Ghosts and goblins, witches and spooks, the Pike house has all kinds of kooks — ' "

"Make her stop!" cried Margo, covering her ears. "I already heard it five times, and I'm sick of it!"

"You're not going to throw up, are you, Margo?" asked Abby. Margo, who is seven, has a weak stomach.

"Not if she quits reading that dumb poem," Margo said.

"I like it," Claire piped up.

"That's because you love witches and ghosts," said Abby, who had heard about the way Claire loves to dress up in her witch's costume. Claire is five, the youngest of the Pike kids.

"Yeah! Ghosts!" Claire cried. "I ain't afraid of no ghosts," she sang, mimicking the deep voice of the guy who sings the *Ghostbusters* theme song.

Mal glanced at Abby and rolled her eyes. "They're all obsessed," she said with a sigh. "I can't seem to escape that movie."

"Well, why fight it?" asked Abby. "Maybe today's the perfect day to do some real ghostbusting."

"Yea!" shouted Vanessa.

"Can we?" begged Margo.

"Ghostbusters!" yelled Claire, so loudly that her four brothers ran in to see what was up.

"What's going on?" asked Nicky.

"I have a strong feeling that this house needs to be ghostbusted from top to bottom," said Abby.

"Yea!" yelled Byron.

"Let's do it!" shouted Adam.

"Who you gonna call?" Jordan chanted.

"GHOSTBUSTERS!" yelled all the kids at once.

"Okay, okay, let's calm down just a little," said Abby, grinning. "First, let's divide up into teams. Mal, if you'll take the younger kids, I'll take Vanessa and the triplets."

"I want to be with Adam and Jordan and Byron!" yelled Nicky immediately.

"And I want to be with my sisters!" said Vanessa. "Who wants to do ghostbusting with you stinky old boys?"

"Okay, so you two can switch teams," said Abby, unruffled. "Now, I think Mal's team can search the basement and the first floor, and my team can check out the attic and the upstairs. Does that sound good?"

36

"Perfect," said Mal, who was enjoying the way Abby had taken charge. She told us later that Abby seemed to have found the perfect balance between being a baby-sitter and a pal. She was ready to have a great time playing with the kids, but she was also careful to organize activities and to keep the situation from becoming too wild.

"Let's head out," said Byron, shouldering his ray gun.

"Hold on, buddy," said Abby. "Not so fast. First, we'd better do an equipment check. Does each team have their ghost detector all charged up?"

The kids looked at each other, bewildered.

"And what about your collection units?" she asked.

The kids looked even more confused. Abby grinned. "Don't have any?" she asked. "No problem. Who got new shoes for school this fall?"

Byron, Nicky, Margo, and Claire raised their hands.

"Still have the boxes?" Abby asked.

They nodded.

"Run and find them," she said. "We'll have our equipment ready in a second."

Sure enough, it didn't take long to transform the shoeboxes with markers and stickers, and attach straps made of string, using plenty of tape. As soon as they were finished, Abby helped two kids on each team put the boxes on, backpack style. "Cool!" she said. "Now we're all set. Let's see which team can catch more ghosts. Ready? *Go!*" She dashed up the stairs, leading her team.

Mal told us later that the rest of the afternoon flew by. The Pike house practically shook with crashes and bangs and shouts, but no permanent damage was done, and the kids had a terrific time.

Mal led her team through the downstairs and into the basement, helping them corner and capture various "ghosts" as they came across them.

"Here's a laundry ghost!" called Claire, opening the dryer door. "Catch him, quick!"

Vanessa scooped the "ghost" into her collection unit.

"There's some ectoplasm dripping down this wall!" yelled Margo.

"Take a sample," Mal told her. "We'll analyze it later, in the lab."

Meanwhile, upstairs, things were a little wilder. Mal heard the shrieks and screams, but she didn't learn the details until later, when Nicky and the triplets filled her in.

First, Abby led the boys on a search of the upstairs bedrooms. They entered each room like a police SWAT team, pushing the door open with their weapons at the ready.

"Remember, never cross the streams!" Abby shouted as they fired at a "ghost" in their parents' room. "That could really mess things up."

The team collected closet ghosts, bathroom ghosts, under-the-bed ghosts, and sock-drawer ghosts until Abby declared the upstairs "free of ghostly presences." Then they headed for the attic stairs.

Abby stopped at the bottom of the stairs. "Give me the ghost detector," she told Byron.

He unslung the shoebox from his shoulder and handed it over.

Abby "took a reading" and pretended to inspect the dials. "Just as I suspected," she said. "The readings are extremely high. Better let me go up first, on my own. I'll call you as soon as I'm sure it's safe." She held up the flashlight she'd been carrying. "Don't worry about me," she said bravely. "I have my weapon charged." She fished a surgical mask out of her pocket (she wears one whenever she might run into dust) and put it on, which made her look even more official. Then she headed up the stairs.

The boys waited for a few seconds. No sound came from above. They waited a few seconds more, expecting Abby to call them any minute. They heard a loud thump, and then there was nothing but silence.

"Abby?" Adam finally called in a quavery voice.

"Are you okay?" Jordan added.

"We'd better go up after her," said Byron uncertainly.

"Do you think something — you know — *caught* her?" Nicky asked.

"I'm going to check," said Adam, trying to sound firm. "You guys coming?"

"Of course," Jordan replied.

"Sure," said Byron, adjusting his weapon.

"Yup," said Nicky.

"Okay, let's go!" Adam cried. He led the charge up the stairs, with the others close behind him.

As the four of them entered the dark attic, Abby sprang out from behind a post, holding the flashlight beneath her chin to give herself a ghoulish appearance. (She'd taken off her mask just for a second.) "Bwah-hah-hah-hah!" she shrieked.

"Aaaaaaaaah!" yelled the boys.

Jordan was the first to catch himself. "It's a ghost!" he hollered. "Watch out! I'm a ghost-buster!" He lifted his weapon and "fired," and the other boys joined in.

Abby turned off the flashlight and slumped to the floor with the moan of a dying ghost, and then she sneezed, and they all cracked up. Ghostbusting had never been so much fun.

CHAPTER 5

"Mischief Knights?"

"What are the Mischief Knights?"

"*Who* are the Mischief Knights, and what are they going to do next?"

Those were the questions everybody was asking on Monday. That day will definitely go down in SMS history: the day the Mischief Knights first struck. I know I'll never forget it, and I have a feeling that SMS students will be talking about that day, and about the Mischief Knights, for years to come.

For me, it started when I was at my locker before homeroom on Monday. It was taking me a long time to wake up that morning. You know how that is? On some days you jump out of bed and plunge right into your routine, but on others you just feel as if you're in a fog for half the day. Well, that morning the fog was as thick and heavy as pea soup. I wasn't thrilled about being at school. All I wanted to do was run back home, jump into bed, and snuggle under the covers.

Instead, I was rummaging around in my locker, trying to find the books I would need for that morning's classes. And then, through the fog, I began to realize that something wasn't right. The books I needed weren't there.

"What's going on?" I heard someone ask. Which was exactly what I had been about to say.

I closed my locker door partway and looked around to see who had spoken. It was Sabrina Bouvier, whose locker is about five lockers over from mine. Sabrina is nice enough, but she looks as if she's thirteen going on thirty. (She trowels on the makeup and dresses like an actress on a soap opera.) At that moment, she peered at me. Her perfectly tweezed brows were mushed together as she frowned. "This isn't my stuff," she said, holding up two textbooks, and a green spiral notebook.

I recognized the notebook immediately. It was my social studies notebook, the one I had been doodling on in homeroom the week before. "That's mine!" I cried, blushing a little when I saw all the hearts I'd drawn. "What's it doing in your locker?"

Sabrina looked bewildered. "I have no idea," she said.

I reached into my locker and pulled out a pile of books. "Are these by any chance yours?" I asked her. Somehow, I just knew they were.

She took two steps toward me. "This is so weird," she said. "How did my stuff find its way into your locker?"

Just then, a folded scrap of white paper fell out of one of her books and drifted to the floor. "What's that?" I asked. I picked it up and unfolded it. This is what I saw:

MISCHIEF KNIGHTS.

I showed it to Sabrina. "What's this all about?" I asked.

She shrugged. "How should I know?" Just then, the first bell rang. "Quick, give me my stuff," she said. I handed it over, and she gave me my books. Then she took off, heading toward the girls' bathroom, probably so she could check her "face" before homeroom.

That was my introduction to the Mischief Knights. But I wasn't the only one meeting them that day. Their handiwork showed up all over SMS, and by lunchtime there wasn't anybody in the school who hadn't heard of them.

"Rick Chow told me they left a message on the blackboard in the music room," Claudia said as she bit into a Ring-Ding she'd pulled out of her backpack.

"What did it say?" asked Mary Anne. She was picking at the grayish slice of Salisbury steak that sat in the middle of her plate.

"It said 'Don't buy the Salisbury steak,' " Kristy joked, poking at the meat on her own plate. "Man, this stuff is disgusting. It reminds me of something Boo-Boo dragged in from the garden." (Boo-Boo is Kristy's stepfather's geriatric cat.)

"Kristy!" Mary Anne said.

"Sorry," Kristy apologized with a grin. She dug into her mashed potatoes. "So what did the message really say?" she asked Claudia.

"Something about how the Mischief Knights couldn't be stopped."

"That's what they wrote on the board in my math class!" said Abby. "Only Mr. Zizmore erased it as soon as he came in, so I didn't really have a good look at it." Abby's eyes were glowing. "Isn't it cool? I love it when something like this gets a school stirred up. In my old school, people used to start rumors, but this is much more fun."

"Fun?" asked Kristy. "Not if you have Mrs. Simon for English. Or at least, not if you had good grades in her class. Which I did."

"Sure you did," I teased her. "If you say so, Kristy." By then, everybody knew that Mrs. Simon's grade book had disappeared that morning, and that a blank one had been put in its place. A tiny scrap of paper with the initials "MK" had been left near the book.

"Mrs. Simon was pretty steamed," Kristy said. "She spent the period lecturing us on why pranks are 'counterproductive.' Meanwhile, the guys in the back row were trying to figure out how to join the Mischief Knights."

"So who do you think they are?" asked Mary Anne.

"I would bet Watson's salary that Alan Gray is involved," Kristy said.

"Don't be so sure," replied Claudia. "I saw him in the hall before, talking to Pete Black. From what I overheard, neither of them knew a thing about the Mischief Knights before today."

"Who, then?" I asked. "Who else would come up with all those pranks?"

"It could be anyone," said Kristy.

"It could be me!" said Abby, waggling her eyebrows.

"Or me," said Mary Anne.

"Oh, right," Kristy said, as we cracked up.

Whoever they were, the Mischief Knights continued their stunts over the next few days. More messages appeared on blackboards. Weird things, such as a rubber chicken or a toilet plunger, appeared in people's lockers. Hundreds of marbles spilled out of a cabinet in the art room when somebody opened it to look for the watercolor paints. Mr. Kingbridge was going nuts. But most of the kids thought the pranks were cool.

The Mischief Knights would have been the most popular kids at SMS, except for one thing; nobody knew who they were. But everybody was talking about them. They even came up at the first meeting of the decorations committee that Wednesday afternoon.

"Maybe we should use the Mischief Knights for a theme," Rick Chow said, practically before we'd found seats.

"I'm not sure that would go over too well with the administration," said a tall, thin man with curly black hair, who was leaning against the blackboard. He smiled at Rick. "I'm sure the students would love it, though."

At that point, he must have noticed that we were looking at him questioningly. "I'm Michael Rothman," he said. "Mr. Rothman, to you. I just started teaching sixth-grade science here at SMS. I've seen a few of you in the halls, but why don't we all introduce ourselves?"

Cokie, naturally, had to be first. "I'm Cokie Mason," she said. "What happened to Mrs. Hall? She was supposed to be our advisor."

I thought Cokie sounded rude, but Mr. Rothman didn't seem to mind. "I ousted her," he said simply. Then he grinned. "Not really. I just asked her if I could be your advisor because I wanted the chance to be involved in helping you plan the dance. Since I'm new here, I figured it would be a good way to become familiar with the school."

Mr. Rothman seemed nice. And he made a good advisor: after we'd introduced ourselves, he sat back and let us talk about what we wanted to do. We came up with a great theme for the dance: The Addams Family Reunion. It was Todd Long's idea, and everybody loved it. Well, everybody except Cokie. She wanted some dumb theme involving jack-o'-lanterns, but we ignored her.

In fact, Cokie was ignored a lot during that meeting. And outvoted. Even Grace disagreed with every single idea Cokie brought up, and Grace is supposed to be Cokie's best friend. I could tell that it especially drove Cokie crazy to see Grace agreeing with me, a BSC member.

(Cokie still hasn't gotten over the fact that Grace teamed up with the BSC to solve a mystery recently, while Cokie was sick with bronchitis.)

I brought up my idea about a red and purple color scheme. "Because orange and black is so tired," I explained.

"Orange and black is *traditional*," Cokie said.

"So what?" Rick asked. "Stacey's right. Why do things the same way all the time?"

"I love the idea of red and purple," said Grace. "It'll look kind of spooky and gothic and bloody."

"Whoever heard of purple for Halloween?" Cokie muttered.

"Are we reaching a consensus here about colors?" asked Mr. Rothman. He sounded just a tiny bit nervous. Maybe he thought we were about to start squabbling. But there was no need for argument. Since everybody but Cokie loved my color scheme, the majority ruled.

The majority also ruled when we started to talk about decorations. We decided to poke around in antique stores and flea markets, looking for Addams Family-type items. (Cokie suggested cutouts of witches, but guess how many of us agreed? Right. Zero.) And we all (except Cokie) agreed that Claudia would be the perfect person to design our advertising posters.

By the end of the meeting, I was pretty excited about the dance, and so were the other committee members. Obviously I wasn't the only one who had decided not to let Cokie ruin what could be a great time.

CHAPTER 6

On Thursday morning, we arrived for classes to find that the Mischief Knights had TP'ed (toilet papered) the entire school. On Thursday afternoon, they soaped the windows of every car left in the teachers' parking lot. Friday morning they sneaked into the main office and made a fake announcement over the loudspeaker about a surprise assembly with "special guest star Michael Jordan." (We spent half of Friday's BSC meeting trying to figure out how they'd pulled that one off.) And on the following Monday morning they set all the classroom clocks ahead by fifteen minutes.

On Monday afternoon, I arrived early for a decorations committee meeting and found Mr. Rothman kneeling by the door, busy with a roll of paper towels and a bottle of Fantastik. There was a familiar smell in the air. I sniffed, trying to place it. "Peanut butter?" I guessed.

He grinned and nodded. "On the doorknob.

And on my shirt and my pants after I touched the doorknob."

"The Mischief Knights?" I asked. I was glad that he seemed to be taking the prank well. Some of the teachers were becoming pretty cranky about the Mischief Knights, especially after Thursday's window-soaping episode.

Mr. Rothman nodded. "They left their mark," he said, pointing to a smeared "MK" written in peanut butter above the doorknob. He smiled and shook his head. "I can't believe I was taken in by this trick. I did it to one of *my* teachers when I was in — let's see — seventh grade, I think."

I tried to imagine Mr. Rothman in seventh grade and decided he probably would have looked pretty geeky, with that tall, lanky frame. I smiled to myself. Just then, somebody grabbed my arm and pulled me into the room.

"I have to talk to you," hissed Cokie.

"Huh?"

"Quick, before Grace gets here," she said, glancing toward the door nervously.

"What's up?" I asked. I couldn't even begin to imagine what Cokie wanted to talk to me about.

"It's about Grace," Cokie whispered, shaking her hair back from her face. "You know how she's been bragging about that boy she's going to bring to the dance?"

"I might have heard her mention him," I said, confused. "So?"

"So I'm not convinced he exists," said Cokie, raising her eyebrows.

"Cokie, what are you talking about?" I asked.

"Okay, he's supposed to be from Lawrenceville, right? And she met him through her cousin? Fine. But why doesn't she have any pictures of him?"

"Well, if they just met — " I began, but Cokie cut me off.

"Not to mention that every time she describes him he sounds different. Like, the other day she said he had green eyes, but the week before she told me hazel."

"Big deal!" I said. "Green and hazel are pretty close."

"Okay," she said. "How about this, then? Ten minutes ago, when we were at her locker, Grace showed me a letter she supposedly received from this guy. Ted, his name is."

"And?" What was Cokie driving at?

"Well, 'Ted's' handwriting looks an awful lot like Grace's. Think about it." She leaned back and crossed her arms.

"Cokie, I just want to know one thing," I said, exasperated. "Why are you telling *me* all of this?"

"Because, for some bizarre reason, Grace

likes you," she answered. "And I thought you kind of liked her, too. I'm worried about her. What's she going to do when the night of the dance arrives and she can't produce this Ted? She'll never live it down."

Right, because you won't let her, I thought. But I didn't say anything out loud, since just then Grace herself walked in. I looked her over carefully, as if I could discover by her appearance whether Cokie was right or not. But Grace looked like her normal self. She was wearing thermal leggings and a blue plaid flannel shirt, and when she plopped herself down on a chair near Cokie and me she let out a big sigh.

"I hope we're not doing all of this work for nothing," she said.

Immediately, I forgot about the mystery of Ted. "What?" I asked.

"My mom says that the school board might call off the dance if community pressure keeps building."

"Oh, you mean because of those letters to the editor?" Cokie asked. "But that's just one old crank."

"Mr. — Mr. Wetzler," I said, recalling the name. "I've seen those letters." We all had. This nutty guy had been writing letters to the editor of the *Stoneybrook News*, protesting our dance and a whole bunch of other stuff in the school budget.

" 'Why should honest citizens pay so that teenagers can cavort in a gym, risking another tragedy?' " Cokie said mockingly. She was quoting one of the letters.

" 'Social studies and science? Yes! Shindigs? No!,' " I said, quoting one of the protest signs I'd seen in what I figured was Mr. Wetzler's yard, which I pass on my way to school every day. We laughed. "Don't worry, Grace," I assured her. "Nobody's going to take that nut seriously. I mean, *tragedy*? What's he talking about?"

"I don't know," she said, sighing. "He's just one more thing to worry about."

"What else are you worried about?" I asked, leaning forward. Maybe Cokie was right, after all.

"I don't know," she said. "I think the pressure of finding a date for the dance can be pretty tough on some kids." She bent down to pull something out of her backpack.

Cokie and I exchanged glances over Grace's head. Cokie gave me an "I told you so" look.

"I overheard some seventh-grade boys talking about how they could never work up the nerve to ask somebody to the dance," Grace said, straightening up.

"Hmmm," I murmured. Whether or not Grace was actually talking about herself, this was an issue we should deal with. "Maybe we should make sure our posters say it's fine to come alone."

"Oh, right!" said Cokie, laughing. "Who wants to come to a dance alone?"

"I would," said Rick Chow, who had just joined us.

"So would I," said Grace. "That is, if Ted weren't coming with me."

"Not everybody has to have a date," said Todd Long, who had come in right after Rick.

Cokie's face was flaming. Once again, everybody had sided against her. "Okay, fine," she mumbled. "We'll put it on the posters."

"I think that's a capital idea," said Mr. Rothman, who had finally finished cleaning up the peanut butter. "Now, how are the plans for decorations coming?"

"I found a whole bunch of cool old picture frames in my uncle's barn," said Rick. "I was thinking we could make a creepy portrait gallery with them, you know, with fake spider webs draped all over them?"

"Excellent," I said admiringly. "I bet Claudia would love to do some of the portraits. She could probably make them look as if their eyes were following you around."

"I shopped for the basics," Todd reported. "I bought a bunch of red light bulbs and about ten rolls each of purple and red streamers."

"We can store everything in my classroom," said Mr. Rothman. "Anything else?"

"My grandmother has this incredible glass punch bowl," Grace offered. "It's huge, and it looks just like something Morticia would use at a party. Anyway, she said we could borrow it."

"Great," said Todd enthusiastically. "Maybe we can figure out some way to use dry ice so it looks like the punch is smoking. I'll talk to one of the people on the refreshments committee."

By the time our meeting broke up, everybody was excited about our plans for the dance. Except Cokie. She still didn't like the Addams Family theme, but she was stuck with it. As far as the rest of us were concerned, we were beginning to feel as if we were all set for the dance.

That's why it was such a shock when Rick ran to me on Friday morning as I was heading for social studies class.

"Did you hear?" he asked me. His face was pale.

"Hear what?" I asked.

"About what happened to all that stuff Todd bought. You know, the streamers and the light bulbs?"

"What about them?" I asked.

"Gone," said Rick. "The streamers are cut into shreds, and the light bulbs are smashed."

"You're kidding!"

He shook his head. "I wish I was," he said. "Todd is really bummed."

"I don't blame him. Was it the Mischief Knights?"

"If it was, they didn't leave a note or anything. But I don't think it was them. It's not their style."

I nodded. He was right. "But who, then?"

Rick shrugged. "Don't know," he said. "Anyway, I have to run. We'll figure it out at the next meeting." He took off down the hall.

I headed in the opposite direction, walking slowly and thinking hard. Who would want to wreck the decorations?

Suddenly, I had an awful thought. What if Cokie were right about Grace, that Ted really didn't exist? Maybe Grace was trying to sabotage the dance, so she wouldn't be caught in a lie.

I shook my head. It was too ridiculous. Grace would never be so destructive. Would she?

"Nah," I said out loud. And as I walked

into social studies class, I reminded myself not to jump to conclusions. The vandalism was terrible, but it was probably just a one-time thing. Anyway, it would be wrong to blame it on an innocent person.

CHAPTER 7

"So? What do you think?" Claud stood back from her bed, where she'd laid out two of the five huge red-and-purple posters she had made. She had asked me to come to Monday's BSC meeting a little early so she could show them to me.

"They're awesome," I said finally. "They're the best posters I've ever seen." They were, too. When I had asked Claudia if she wanted to help out by making the posters for the dance, I had known she'd do a good job. But I never expected the posters to look as professional and as eye-catching as they did. "These look like something you'd see plastered on a bus in New York," I said. "Like an ad campaign from a top agency."

"Well, you helped design them," Claud pointed out. "You're the mastermind. All I did was follow your orders."

"The whole committee designed them," I

reminded her. "Well, except Cokie. She didn't like this idea."

"She'll like it now, when she sees the posters," Claudia said.

"I wouldn't count on it."

Guess what? I was right. Cokie didn't like the posters. She saw them the next morning, when the decorations committee met half an hour before homeroom in order to hang the posters in the halls.

Rick thought the posters were "incredible."

Todd said they were "wicked."

Grace couldn't believe how "artistic" they were.

Cokie? All she noticed was that Claudia had misspelled "masquerade" on one of the posters.

That made me mad. Claudia had worked hard, and she'd been especially careful about her spelling. You have to understand that for Claud to spell only one word wrong on five posters is pretty close to a miracle. But I didn't say anything to Cokie. I just ignored her, and so did Grace, Rick, and Todd. Using a stepladder borrowed from the janitor, we hung the posters up; two in the halls near the cafeteria, one near the main entrance, one by the gym, and one by the auditorium. They looked amazing.

"This dance is going to be the best!" Grace

said, stepping back after we'd hung the last poster. "Ted's going to be really impressed."

I knew Cokie was giving me one of her Looks behind Grace's back, but I pretended not to see it. "I'm sure he will be," I told Grace. I wanted so badly to believe that there was a Ted, so I wouldn't have to believe that Grace could have destroyed the streamers and light bulbs. Now that I was with her, it was almost impossible to picture her doing such a thing. Grace has such a sweet, honest face.

"Yeah, well, Carrie had a sweet face, too," said Claud as she pulled out a purple marker and started on some careful lettering. "And look what happened at her school!"

I shuddered, remembering. Claudia and I rented the movie, *Carrie*, a few months earlier, and I don't think I slept for a week afterward. I like scary movies, but that one was over the top.

It was Wednesday afternoon, and my friends and I were gathered in Claudia's room for a BSC meeting. But we weren't talking about clients or schedules or any other kind of BSC business. We were talking about the latest bizarre episode at SMS.

Here's how I found out about it: When I arrived at school that Wednesday morning, Todd Long met me near the side door. "You won't believe it," he said. "*I* don't believe it."

"What?" I asked. But Todd wouldn't answer. He just led me through the halls until we were near the cafeteria. The floor was covered with tiny bits of red confetti. "So?" I said. "Somebody made some weird mess here. Is this what you wanted to show me?"

Todd didn't answer. He cast his gaze around at the walls, and I followed it. That's when it hit me. The posters! That wasn't confetti on the floor. It was Claudia's beautiful posters, all ripped into minuscule bits.

I put my hand over my mouth. I couldn't speak.

"I know," Todd said grimly. "They also tore up the one near the auditorium and the one by the main entrance."

"But why?" I asked. "What a horrible thing to do."

"That's not the worst of it," Todd said. "I want you to see something else." He led me through the halls again, this time toward the gym. I had no idea what he was going to show me, but I did know one thing: I probably didn't want to see it.

"Nice, huh?" Todd asked as we rounded the last corner.

I looked up at the poster we'd hung there and drew in a sharp breath.

"At least they left one of them up," Todd

said. He was trying to lighten the situation, but it didn't work. What I was seeing sent chills down my spine, and no amount of joking was going to make those chills go away.

Spray-painted across the poster, in drippy, red, bloody-looking letters was this message:

WILL YOU STILL LOVE ME TOMORROW?

Todd was looking at me, as if he expected me to say something, but I couldn't. I was too creeped out. Instead, I helped him take the poster down and roll it up. We'd have to make more posters — I knew that much — but would they just be ruined too?

Finally, as we walked down the hall toward our lockers (it was nearly time for homeroom), I thought of something. "Do you think it might have been the Mischief Knights?" I asked Todd.

He shook his head slowly. "I almost wish it had been them," he said. "That would make this easier to understand. But if they did it, they sure didn't want anyone to know. They didn't leave a note, or their initials, or anything."

I remembered what Rick had said about the torn-up streamers, that it wasn't the Mischief

Knights' style. I'd thought he was right about that, and the same thing applied here. Ripping up posters isn't mischief; it's vandalism, plain and simple. And writing on them is vandalism also, especially if you're trying to scare people.

And people *would* have been scared, if they'd seen the poster, or heard about what it said. But Todd and I agreed to keep it as quiet as we could. That's why I had waited until the BSC meeting to tell my friends about it, and to show them the poster, which I'd stuck into my backpack after we'd rolled it up.

Claudia was already at work on some new posters — that's what she was doing with the purple marker — while we talked about what had happened and tried to guess who had done it.

Claudia had a suspect in mind. "Little Ms. Mason," she said angrily. "Face it, she never liked my posters to begin with. I wouldn't put it past Cokie to take advantage of the fact that all those pranks have been happening at school. She knew she could do some vandalism and blame it on the Mischief Knights."

"I don't know," Kristy said, tapping her pencil against her teeth. "I think the Mischief Knights really might have done it. Maybe that other stuff they did was just for starters."

"You mean they were leading up to bigger things?" asked Abby, from her perch on

Claud's art books. She was playing with one of the Twizzlers Claud had passed around. She had pulled the strands apart, and now she was braiding them back together.

"Right," said Kristy. "Just when everybody was starting to enjoy their fun and games — wham!"

"What about Grace?" Jessi asked. She was talking into the floor as she did one of her painful-looking ballet stretches. "Is she still a suspect, Stace?"

"Well, I don't know," I said. "It really seems unlikely. She's just too sweet, even if she is Cokie's best friend. I can't imagine her tearing into those posters."

"But *somebody* did it," Mal said. "And whoever it is probably looks just as sweet as Grace. But underneath, he — or she — is different."

"Oohh, creepy," said Abby, grinning. "I'll never look at my classmates the same way again. I'll always be wondering about that nasty 'underneath' part."

"You don't have to look far, with Cokie," Claudia muttered.

"What about the streamers and the light bulbs, though?" I asked. "Why would Cokie have ruined them?"

Claudia gave me a Look. "Come on, Stacey," she said. "Think about it."

I knew the answer almost before she finished speaking. "Because she hated the color scheme," I said slowly. Claudia nodded triumphantly.

"But is that really a reason for doing such a terrible thing?" Mary Anne asked suddenly. We all turned to look at her, and she blushed. She had been quiet during our meeting so far. "I've been thinking," she continued. "Maybe we're limiting ourselves by only looking for suspects at SMS."

"Where else should we look?" Kristy asked.

"Well, we could look in the community," Mary Anne said in a small voice. Then she sat up straight, and her voice became stronger. "We could look at Mr. Wetzler."

I gasped. "Mr. Wetzler! Sure! He's a definite suspect. Good thinking, Mary Anne."

Our meeting broke up soon after that, even though we hadn't come up with any answers. But less than twenty-four hours later, we were back in Claudia's room for an emergency meeting and we were talking about suspects again. Why? Because there had been another act of vandalism at the school. Somebody went wild with the red spray paint again, only this time it wasn't on a poster. It was on the walls of the gym. Here's what it said:

$10

That's all. $10. In figures about eight feet high. Nobody had a clue what it meant. Especially Mr. Kingbridge, who made a special announcement to plead for an end to the vandalism, and to tell us that he might cancel the dance if it didn't stop. That's why Kristy called the meeting.

"Okay," she'd said as soon as we had gathered in Claudia's room after school. "We have a genuine mystery on our hands. And the BSC never leaves a mystery unsolved, right?" She looked around expectantly.

"Right!" we replied.

"Right," Kristy echoed. "Let's do it. We don't want this dance to be canceled, do we?"

"No way," said Claud, pulling out a notebook. "Let's start. I'll make a list of suspects."

After that, we returned to the same discussion we'd had the day before. Only I wasn't contributing to it. I was remembering the "tragedy" Mr. Wetzler had mentioned in one of his wacky letters to the editor. And I was thinking about something Mr. Kingbridge had said when he first announced the dance. He'd mentioned something about "erasing those unpleasant memories of the past." What tragedy? What memories? Somebody seemed determined to make sure the dance never took place — but what if it wasn't someone who went to SMS now? What if it was someone else, someone who remembered something awful about the last Halloween masquerade, twenty-eight years ago?

CHAPTER 8

Thursday

Who would have thouhgt that a pair
of eigth-year-olds and an eighth grader
coud take on a real gohst and win? Well
beleive it becuase its true. Those Arnold
girls are the best little gohstbusters I ever saw.

As soon as our emergency meeting ended, Claudia dashed over to the Arnolds' for a sitting job. She arrived at two minutes to five: two minutes early. Mr. and Mrs. Arnold were driving to Stamford for dinner with Mr. Arnold's boss, so Claud would sit for the eight-year-old Arnold twins, Carolyn and Marilyn, from five until around nine. That meant Claudia would be giving the girls dinner, which was fine with Claudia, since she hadn't had a chance to grab a bite. Mrs. Arnold always leaves plenty of good food and urges her sitters to eat as much as they like.

Claudia smiled to herself as she walked to the Arnolds' door. A life-sized skeleton (with glowing eyes) dangled from the porch ceiling, and four carved jack-o'-lanterns with toothy, jagged smiles decorated the porch stairs. A string of orange pumpkin lights outlined the front door, and there were white ghost and black cat cutouts on all the windows. The Arnolds love to decorate their house for holidays. You should see it at Christmastime.

Mrs. Arnold answered the door when Claudia rang the bell. She looked elegant in her black velvet skirt and white satin blouse.

"Love the jewelry," Claudia said.

"Thanks," Mrs. Arnold replied, smiling as she touched one of her dangly orange ear-

71

rings, which was in the shape of a tiny pumpkin. She also wore a necklace with a pumpkin pendant, and a bracelet with dangling pumpkins. Mrs. Arnold tends to go a little overboard in the accessories department.

Mr. Arnold appeared behind her. "Ready?" he asked as he shrugged into his coat.

Five minutes later, they left and Claudia was headed for the Arnolds' basement rec room. "Carolyn?" she called down the stairs. "Marilyn? Your mom said you were down here. What's up?"

There was no answer.

"Guys?" Claudia called.

Still no answer. Claudia started down the stairs, and soon she spotted the twins. They were hunched over their low art table, working hard on something. It was clear that they were so absorbed in their project that they hadn't even heard her call. "Hi, Carolyn," Claud said. "Hi, Marilyn. What are you guys doing?"

"We're busy!" Carolyn said.

"We have to fix this thing," Marilyn explained.

"Fix *what* thing?" Claudia asked, trying to peek at what they were working on.

The twins exchanged serious glances, and Claudia was struck all over again by with how much they look alike. When we first met the twins, we had trouble telling them apart. We had to remember that Marilyn was the one with the tiny mole beneath her right eye, and that Carolyn had a similar mole under her left eye. Back then, Mrs. Arnold was dressing the girls alike, and they shared a room. Over time, though, they've begun to express their separate personalities. Now they have their own rooms, and each room is decorated differently. They have different hair styles (Carolyn's is much trendier), different ways of dressing (Marilyn wears simpler clothes), and totally different interests. (For example, Marilyn is a dedicated piano student, while Carolyn, who is tone-deaf, is fascinated with science.) As you can imagine, we no longer have any trouble telling them apart.

The twins are very close, though. Sometimes, when they want to exclude other kids (or sitters), they communicate in a made-up language no one else understands. And they often communicate without speaking at all. That's what they were doing down in the basement that afternoon, as Claudia waited to find out what they were up to. They looked into each other's eyes for just a few seconds, then they nodded and Marilyn said, "Come see!"

Claudia moved forward to take a look. She saw a board with wires and flashing lights. Attached to it was a funnel, and attached to that was a flashlight. "Cool!" she said. "What is it?"

"A ghost-finder," Marilyn said.

"Marilyn," said Carolyn sternly. "It's not a 'ghost-finder.' It's an ectoplasmic turbulence detector."

Claudia nodded. Suddenly it was all clear. The Arnold twins had been watching *Ghostbusters*, too.

"She invented it," Marilyn said proudly, pointing to her sister.

"I had to," Carolyn explained. "It was an emergency."

"What do you mean?" asked Claudia.

"We have a ghost," Carolyn answered.

"In this house," Marilyn added. "We started hearing it last week, and we've heard it every day since then."

"Uh-huh," Claudia said with a smile. She knows the twins have very active imaginations. "Is the ghost by any chance friends with Gozzie Kunka?" Gozzie Kunka used to be Marilyn's imaginary friend. "Or is it something that arrived here through your time machine?" she asked, turning to Carolyn.

"Gozzie Kunka isn't an actual person," said Marilyn impatiently.

"And the time machine was just for fun," said Carolyn. "This ghost isn't imaginary or pretend. It's real. And as soon as we can take a reading on it and find out what type of apparition it is, we can figure out how to catch it."

Claudia was interested. "You say you've heard this ghost?"

"Definitely," said Carolyn.

"It makes horrible sounds, like something trying to claw its way out of a coffin," said Marilyn.

"Have you told your parents about the noises?" asked Claudia.

The twins nodded. "I told Mom last night," said Marilyn. "She said I couldn't watch *Ghostbusters* anymore."

"And I told Dad at breakfast this morning," Carolyn said. "He said it was all probably a dream. But it isn't. I know it isn't. The noises are real, and so is the ghost, and we're going to do something about it." She looked defiant.

"Well, okay," said Claudia. "Fine with me." She could tell the girls were serious, and, as she told us later, there didn't seem to be any point in trying to talk them out of busting their ghost. "Where do we start?"

"In my room," said Marilyn promptly. "I heard the sound in there this morning."

"The detector is ready," said Carolyn, checking a few wires. "Let's go!"

The three of them headed upstairs. Marilyn led them into her room, which is very yellow:

the bedspread, the carpet, and the wallpaper are all the same sunny shade. It seemed, according to Claudia, an unlikely setting for "ectoplasmic activity."

But Carolyn set to work, walking around the perimeter of the room with her detector. She looked deadly serious as she aimed the flashlight-funnel attachment this way and that and monitored the flashing lights. Marilyn, meanwhile, followed her sister, pressing her ear to the wall every few steps in order to listen for the ghostly noises.

Claudia sat on the bed, watching them and thinking about how cute they looked. Ghostbuster fever was spreading: first the Pikes (she had read Abby's and Mal's notebook entry) and now the Arnolds. But it seemed harmless, and the kids were having a lot of fun with it, so why not play along?

Suddenly, just as she'd passed the closet door, Carolyn stopped in her tracks. Marilyn nearly bumped into her, but she stopped, too. Claudia noticed the girls' eyes had widened. "What is it?" she asked.

"The ghost," whispered Carolyn. "I hear it."

"So do I," said Marilyn.

Claudia smiled. "Do you have a reading on your detector?" she asked. She joined the girls, and as she drew closer she noticed that

Carolyn had let the detector fall to her side, and that Marilyn's face was much paler than it had been only a few moments before. Suddenly, she realized that the girls were serious. She pressed her ear against the wall and listened. Then *her* eyes widened, too. "Oh, my lord!" she gasped. "I hear it!" She listened carefully, and heard a scratching and clawing sound. Visions of long, clawlike fingernails flashed into Claudia's mind. For a second, she felt panic rising within her. Then she remembered that she was the baby-sitter, and that she was responsible for the girls. It wouldn't do to lose her head. She took a deep breath. "It must be just some branches brushing against the house," she told the twins.

"There's no tree on that side," Carolyn said.

"Maybe it's the wind," Claudia suggested.

"There's no wind today," said Marilyn.

"Could it be the house settling?" Claudia asked hopefully.

"Nope," said Marilyn. "I know what that sounds like. My dad explained that, once when I heard scary creaking noises at night. This is nothing like that."

Each of them put an ear against the wall again and listened. Finally, Claudia gulped. "It's moving," she said. "Now it sounds as if it's coming from high up. Is the attic above this room?"

The girls nodded.

"I'm going to go up and check things out," said Claudia. "Where are the stairs?"

"I'll show you," said Carolyn. She ran out of the room, and Claudia and Marilyn followed.

"We'll come with you," Marilyn offered, when the three of them stood at the bottom of the stairs.

"No," said Claudia. She was feeling more than slightly terrified, but she knew this was something she had to do on her own. "You two wait down here. But can I borrow your flashlight?"

Carolyn detached the flashlight from her detector and handed it over. "Be careful," she said solemnly.

"I will be," Claudia answered. Then she turned and headed up the stairs, flashlight at the ready.

"I would have hated to be the girls at that point," she told us later. "All they saw was me disappearing up the stairs. But then, a few seconds later, they heard me scream. They must have been scared out of their wits. So was I. When I saw those eyes staring back at me I nearly passed out!"

Luckily, Claudia did not pass out. Instead, she shone the flashlight at the eyes and caught sight, just in time, of a fat, gray squirrel as it turned to run out of a hole in the eaves of the roof. After that scare, I don't know how she had the presence of mind to stick a piece of cardboard over the hole, but she did, and the squirrel was locked out, at least temporarily. (The Arnolds could deal with it in the morning.)

After a comforting dinner of macaroni and cheese, Claudia spent the rest of the evening helping the girls make "Professional Ghostbuster" signs for their doors. Then she made one for her own door. The three of them were pretty proud of themselves. After all, it's not every day you actually bust a ghost!

CHAPTER 9

"Twenty-eight *years* ago?" Sharon, Mary Anne's stepmother, raised her eyebrows. "You're asking a lot. I can't even remember what I had for dinner last night."

Mary Anne and I looked at each other and raised our eyebrows. I had to work hard to stifle a grin. Sharon can sometimes be a bit of a flake. It's true that she's a wonderful, smart, loving person. It's also true that she's not very organized, and she's always losing her keys or forgetting to turn on the oven when she's baking potatoes.

While Claud was sitting for the Arnolds that Thursday evening, Mary Anne, Logan, and I had gone to Mary Anne's house after our emergency meeting. Why? Because I had blurted out my theory that the vandalism at school might have something to do with that last Mischief Night dance twenty-eight years earlier. Mary Anne had picked up on the idea immediately, and pointed out that her dad and stepmother had both lived in Stoneybrook at that time and might remember something about the dance. So there we were, sitting in the living room, asking questions.

"I remember plenty of dances in high school," said Mary Anne's dad, smiling softly at Sharon, as if he were remembering romantic moments the two of them had shared long ago. "But middle school? I don't remember going to many dances at all, and I certainly don't remember anything 'tragic' happening at a dance."

"Are you sure?" Mary Anne pressed. "This would have been a Halloween dance, or at least a Mischief Night dance."

"Halloween . . . you know, I do remember something," Sharon began slowly. "Richard, wasn't there a dance once where a teacher was hurt?" She frowned. "Or even killed?"

Mary Anne, Logan, and I exchanged glances.

"A teacher was *killed*?" I asked.

"Mr. Green, wasn't it?" Richard said in a far-off voice. "You're right, Sharon. I *do* remember something, but it's hazy. I know I wasn't at the dance. I would only have been in — let's see — sixth grade, and most dances back then were for the older kids."

"So what happened?" asked Mary Anne, urging her father along.

"You know, I'm really not sure," he said. "I'm trying to remember, but not much is coming back. Something happened, and that teacher — Mr. Green? — died because of it. But I can't recall what it was."

We swiveled to look at Sharon. She shook her head. "I can't remember either," she said. "It was pretty terrible, though. I seem to recall girls crying in the halls." She closed her eyes for a moment, and I could tell she was thinking as hard as she could. Then her eyes popped open. "But Richard, you're wrong about the teacher's name. It wasn't Mr. Green. It was Mr. — Mr. Brown."

"That's it!" he cried. "Mr. Brown. Absolutely. Now that you say it, I know that's right."

"Mr. Brown," I said, making a note in the little notebook I had brought with me. "Wow, thanks for your help. Now that we know something really did happen, maybe we can find out more about the specifics."

"But how?" asked Logan.

"Maybe we could find some old issues of the SMS Express," Mary Anne began, but her father started shaking his head.

"You won't find any old enough," he said.

"The school didn't have a paper then."

"But the town did," Logan said. He glanced at his watch. "If we hurry, we can make it to the library before closing time and look through some old issues of the *Stoneybrook News*." He stood up, and so did Mary Anne and I.

"Let us know what you find out," said Richard. "Now I'm curious, too."

We left Mary Anne's at a trot, and kept it up all the way to the library. I already had a strong feeling we were onto something. If a teacher at SMS had actually died at that dance twenty-eight years ago, well, that was big stuff. I still didn't know exactly what we were looking for, but it seemed clear that we needed to find out as much as we could about that dance.

When we arrived at the library, we headed for the reference room and for the microfilm of the back issues of the *Stoneybrook News*. It wasn't hard to find the spool for October and November of twenty-eight years back. We've used microfilm before, when we were working on other mysteries, so we're pretty good at looking up subjects.

Logan worked the microfilm reader, while Mary Anne and I leaned over his shoulders, scanning quickly. Suddenly, I spotted something that made my heart race. "Stop!" I said.

"What's that?" I pointed to an obituary head-line dated November first. "Educator Jack R. Brown, 62, Died During Stampede."

"*Stampede?*" Mary Anne and Logan asked together. We leaned forward to read the text of the obituary.

"This has to be the guy," Logan said. "It says he was a civics teacher at SMS. And it gives the date of his death as October thir-tieth."

"He died of a heart attack," Mary Anne said, as she read ahead. "And doctors think it was brought on by the 'unfortunate incident' at the school dance."

"The stampede," I repeated. "*What* stam-pede?"

"There must be an article about it some-where," Logan said. He started scanning again.

"Whoa! Stop!" Mary Anne cried. "Check it out." She pointed to the screen, and we saw the headline, which was in a paper dated Oc-tober 31st, Halloween. "Masquerade Takes Tragic Turn," we read out loud, together. Then we read silently, as fast as we could.

Here's what we found out: There was a Hal-loween masquerade that year, and it was held on the night before Halloween, Mischief Night. Attendance was high; most of the eighth grade was there. A band called The

Groovy Tangerine was playing. Suddenly, the lights went out in the gym — and in the whole school. The crowd panicked. Somebody pulled a fire alarm, which caused even more panic, and then a stampede. Several students were injured, and Mr. Brown suffered a heart attack and died before he could be taken to the hospital.

The police believed the blackout was a prank, and that the fire alarm might have been pulled as a prank as well. They questioned many of the students at the dance, and found out that several members of the SMS football team might have been involved. But the police had no proof, and it was likely that the investigation would go no further. The chief of police was quoted as saying he was positive that certain students — they weren't identified by name — knew exactly what had happened, and that he wished they would come forward.

"Wow," breathed Mary Anne.

"Wow is right," Logan said. "This is wild. I never expected to find anything quite this — quite this serious."

"Let's see if there are any follow-up articles," I suggested, and Logan started scanning again.

But we didn't find a thing. It seemed as if the police hadn't been given any information, and the matter had been dropped.

"Now that we know this much, what next?" asked Logan. "We still have a long way to go if we want to find out who's trying to ruin our dance."

"Yearbooks!" I said, snapping my fingers. "Let's go to the school library at lunchtime tomorrow and look through yearbooks from back then. We might find something interesting."

"Keep turning the pages," Kristy said impatiently, as she looked over my shoulder. She'd been excited to hear what we'd found out so far, and so had the other BSC members. We had gathered in the library at lunchtime (all except Jessi and Mal, that is, since the sixth-graders eat lunch at a different time), and we'd found the old yearbook from the year of the dance.

I was holding it, and everyone else had gathered around. I was turning the pages especially slowly, making sure not to miss anything, but I turned a little faster when Kristy said that. Suddenly, I stopped and let out a gasp.

"What?" asked Mary Anne. She moved closer, so that she could see better. "Oh!" she said, echoing my gasp.

We were looking at a full-page picture of an older man in a suit. At the bottom, within a black border, were the words, "In Memory of Mr. Brown."

"That's him," said Mary Anne. Everyone clustered around to look at the picture.

"I bet he was strict," said Claudia. "Doesn't he look it?"

He did. His mouth was a straight line, and his eyes, behind black-framed eyeglasses, looked serious.

"What if he's the one tearing up posters and painting on the walls?" Abby said.

"He's *dead*!" cried Kristy.

"I know," Abby said, with a tiny smile. "But maybe he's not totally dead, if you know what I mean. Maybe he's haunting the school, because his murder was never solved." She raised her eyebrows.

"Stop!" cried Mary Anne. "You're creeping me out. Stacey, turn the page. I can't stand the way he's looking at me."

I turned the page, and we started looking at the eighth-grade pictures. Immediately, we forgot about Abby's ghoulish idea. The pictures were hilarious. "All the boys look so geeky!" cried Kristy. "Look at those haircuts."

"And the girls have such big hair," Claudia said. "How about those cat-eye glasses, too?"

We paged through the pictures, laughing at how strange the kids looked. The funny thing was that they didn't really look like kids at all.

They looked like miniature grown-ups. The boys had short hair and wore suits and ties, and the girls looked as if they were about thirty. I kept turning pages.

"Whoa," I said suddenly, looking at one of the pictures more closely. "Check it out!" I pointed to a picture in the upper left hand corner of the page, of a relatively cute but still geeky-looking guy with black, curly hair.

"What about him?" asked Kristy.

"Look at the name," I said. Underneath the picture, the caption read "Michael Rothman."

"How weird. That's the name of the teacher who's advising the decorations committee." I bent to give the picture a closer look. "Wouldn't it be wild if this was really him, twenty-eight years ago? I didn't know he went to SMS. But it could be him. He's still just as skinny, and he has that black, curly hair." I stared at the picture. I couldn't believe my eyes.

Mary Anne was looking, too, but Abby and Kristy had already shifted their attention to another picture in the lower righthand corner of the page. "What do you think?" asked Kristy. Abby shrugged.

"Who's that?" I asked. Kristy pointed to the name, and I read it out loud. "Jerome Wetzler. Who's that?" Then I remembered, and my eyebrows flew up. "Mr. Wetzler? The guy who's writing all those letters to the editor? Hmmmm."

"Hmmm is right," said Mary Anne. "I second that hmm!"

This was becoming very, very interesting. And it became even more so when we discovered, in the back of the yearbook, pictures of all the athletic teams. Underneath the picture of the football team, we found the name M. Rothman. If this M. Rothman was the M. Rothman I knew, it could be very significant that he was on the football team, since members of the team were suspected of being involved in the prank on the night of the dance.

I leaned forward to examine the picture more closely, and just then the loudspeaker over the library's door crackled to life. "Attention, students," someone said. It sounded sort of like Mr. Kingbridge, but it was hard to tell because of the static. "At the sound of the next bell, students in all grades are to proceed to the auditorium for a special assembly."

CHAPTER 10

When the announcement was over, Claudia giggled. "Mischief Knights again," she guessed.

But she was wrong. As soon as the bell rang, the librarian shooed us out and told us to head straight for the auditorium. "Mr. Kingbridge wants everybody there," she said.

"What's the assembly about?" I asked.

She shrugged. "Your guess is as good as mine."

I wondered if the assembly had anything to do with the dance. "Maybe he's canceling it," I said as my friends and we walked to the auditorium. I didn't have to even explain what I meant by "it." The dance was on everybody's mind.

But, as it turned out, the assembly wasn't about the dance at all. It was a special presentation by a community theatre group, about how to say no when your friends try to talk you into doing things you don't want to do. We've already heard a lot about that, and I actually had to *do* it (say no), once when Sheila and her friends were trying to talk me into drinking at this concert we went to. So I thought I'd be bored. But the skits they performed turned out to be pretty funny, and soon everyone in the auditorium was laughing.

Since this was a special assembly, we could sit wherever we wanted. The BSC members had claimed a row in the back of the left side of the auditorium, and no teachers were nearby. Ordinarily, we might have talked and giggled, but the theatre group grabbed our attention. I was sitting between Claudia and Jessi, near the aisle, so I had a good view of the audience and of the stage.

I especially liked one actress. She had a kind of glow, as if she really loved what she was doing. She was pretty, with big, expressive eyes and a head full of red-gold curls. Plus, she was funny. She was great at the slapstick stuff, such as falls and double takes. I watched her closely, daydreaming a little about what it would be like to act professionally.

When the lights went out, I first thought it was part of the performance.

Then people started to scream, and I realized that *all* the lights were out in the auditorium. Instantly, I remembered what we'd found out the night before, and I felt fear rise inside me. This was like some kind of sick joke, a flashback to that night twenty-eight years earlier when the lights went out in the gym — and a person died.

I felt somebody grab my hand. It was Claudia. We peered at each other through the darkness, and I could tell that she was thinking the same thing I was. I reached out for Jessi's hand, too, and we all held tight.

"Please, please, please! Let's not panic!" That was Mr. Kingbridge's voice. But his plea came too late. Plenty of students were already past the point of being calmed.

Q: How many middle school students does it take to create a stampede?

A: Not many.

I think it started in the front rows, with a group of sixth-graders who were afraid they wouldn't be able to leave the auditorium. Then it grew and grew, until a huge mass of kids was trying to work their way up the aisles. I heard shrieking and yelling and crying, and then a crash and a long scream, from the front of the auditorium. Claudia's hand tightened around mine. We were still sitting there, waiting to see what was going to happen next.

"What was that?" Jessi whispered. She tightened her grip, too.

"I don't know, but it didn't sound good," I whispered back.

Mr. Kingbridge was still trying to calm everybody. But the panic just seemed to spread. I was too afraid to move, so I stayed in my seat. I couldn't see a thing in the dark, and I knew it would be crazy to try to find my way out of the auditorium.

Then, just as suddenly as the lights had gone off, they came back on. Everybody seemed to freeze in place. I saw kids practically piled on top of one another in the aisles, many with flushed, frightened-looking faces. The teachers looked terrified as they tried to herd everyone back to their seats. Mr. Kingbridge jumped off the stage and bent down to look at something, then stood up and called for help. I stood to try to see what was happening, but too many people were in my way.

"What a mess!" I heard Kristy say.

"Was it the Mischief Knights, do you think?" Mal asked.

"No way," said Logan. "They'd have to be nuts to do something as dangerous as this. They're mischievous, but they're not crazy."

I saw a teacher run up the aisle from where Mr. Kingbridge was standing, and out the door. Minutes later, I heard an ambulance siren. Once again, I felt the fear rise. What if it had happened again? What if somebody had had a heart attack?

Mr. Kingbridge climbed back onto the stage. "Okay, people, let's just stay calm. I don't think we have any major injuries here, although it looks as if one of our actresses has been hurt. The emergency medical people will take care of her, and they'll check out anyone else who believes they're injured. In the meantime, I'd like the rest of you to leave the auditorium — in an orderly fashion — and proceed to your eighth-period classes."

The assembly was over. I found out later that the actress I had liked, the one with red hair, had fallen off the stage (that was the scream I'd heard) and broken her arm. I also found out later that nobody had a good explanation for why the lights had gone out. The Mischief Knights did not claim responsibility, and nobody else did, either. Was it an accident, or a prank? Nobody knew. But I, and the other BSC members, suspected that the episode was somehow connected to the mystery, and we decided to step up our efforts. If we didn't solve the mystery soon, somebody might *really* get hurt . . . or even killed. It was time to follow up every possible clue we had.

That's how I ended up interviewing Mr. Wetzler.

Now, I'm not usually a very good liar. Still,

in this case, I thought the situation called for a tiny fib. After all, what's the best way to find out more about who somebody is and what they know? Interview them. But in order to do an interview, you have to be a reporter, which I'm not. That's where the fib comes in. When I called Mr. Wetzler, I told him that I was with the *SMS Express*, and that I wanted to ask him some questions about the school budget "and its impact on eighth-graders like me." Since the school budget happens to be his favorite subject, he fell for it hook, line, and sinker. An hour later, I met him at the Rosebud Cafe and we sat down to talk.

I had thought ahead and brought a tape recorder, which turned out to be a great idea. As Mr. Wetzler and I sipped tea and chatted, the tape recorder did the work. I didn't have to remember anything. All I had to do later was listen to the tapes and transcribe what we said. I found out some very interesting things, but somehow I didn't think Mr. Wetzler was telling me everything he knew. You can judge for yourself; here's the interview. Mr. Wetzler is JW (for Jerry Wetzler, of course), and you know who SM is.

SM: Thank you for meeting with me today, Mr. Wetzler.

JW: No problem. Hey, is that thing on?

SM: Yes, it is. I record all my interviews. Do you mind?

JW: I guess not.

SM: Let's begin, then. First of all, I understand that you disapprove of the current school budget.

JW: I do, indeed. There's waste everywhere, and my taxes are paying for it.

SM: Waste? For example — ?

JW: Those ridiculous dances, for one. They're totally unnecessary, not to mention dangerous.

SM: Dangerous? Are you by any chance referring to the *last* Halloween masquerade twenty-eight years ago?

JW: That's right.

SM: Can you tell me more about what happened there?

JW: Uh, I don't really —

SM: Details might be helpful, if you are trying to convince the school to cancel future dances.

JW: Well, a teacher died. A Mr. Brown. In a stampede.

SM: What caused the stampede?

JW: I think it had something to do with that eighth-grade girl, the one who was jilted at the dance. She created havoc, and then she disappeared and never came back to school.

SM: *What?* Um, I mean — very interesting.

Can you tell me more about this girl?

JW: No, no. I don't remember anything else. I really don't.

SM: But she never came back?

JW: She never came back.

SM: Why — ?

JW: Oh, my goodness, would you look at the time? I have to go. I — I have dinner plans!

SM: Well — well thanks for your time. If you have more time later, I'd like to ask you more —

JW: I'm afraid that won't be possible.

That's it. There's nothing else on the tape. He left the Rosebud so fast I didn't even have a chance to say good-bye. And the weird thing was that it was only about four o'clock. Why would he have to rush off for dinner at that hour?

It was very interesting, but I couldn't figure out what it meant. This thing about the girl, for example. That was new to me. All I knew was that my friends and I had to keep investigating until we could put the pieces of the puzzle together. And we had to work fast.

CHAPTER 11

"How do you find somebody who isn't there? How do you even start *looking* for somebody who isn't there?"

"What?" Kristy put down her fork and stared at me. "Stacey, what are you babbling about?"

I looked around the table and realized that *all* of my friends were staring at me. I also realized that I must have spoken out loud when I hadn't meant to. I was so caught up in thinking about how to find out more about the girl Mr. Wetzler had mentioned that I'd barely been aware of the fact that I wasn't alone. I was startled to find myself at a table in the SMS cafeteria surrounded by my friends, who were looking at me with concerned expressions. It was the Tuesday before Halloween weekend. We had spent lots of time during the last two BSC meetings trying to understand how what Mr. Wetzler had told me fit into our mystery. But nobody had come up with any answers — yet.

"It's okay, I haven't gone around the bend," I assured them. "I'm just trying to figure something out." I started to peel an orange.

"Well, clue us in," said Abby.

"It's about that girl, the one Mr. Wetzler told me about. That's the first we've heard about a girl being mixed up in what happened at the dance. It just seems like — "

"Like if we can find out more about her, we'd be able to solve the mystery," Claudia finished. She crumpled up an empty Doritos bag and tossed it at me. "Good thinking, Stace!"

"I think it's mean that he seems to blame everything on her," Mary Anne mused. "How could one girl be responsible for a stampede?" She bit into her sandwich thoughfully.

"You never know," said Logan, who was sitting next to her. He had already gulped down a school lunch with double helpings of everything — tacos were on the menu that day — and now he was looking hungrily at Mary Anne's sandwich. She offered him a bite, and he took a big one. "But Stacey's right. No matter what, the first thing we have to do is find the girl."

"But how?" I asked. "We don't even know her name."

"And even if we did, she wouldn't be in the yearbook," said Kristy, "because she left school in the fall."

"Whoa!" Claudia said. "Hold on a second. Hey, Kristy, remember that really cute guy back in sixth grade? The one with the curly blond hair and the *eyes*?" She turned to me. "It was like he had these two laser beams," she explained. "When he looked at you with those blue eyes of his, you'd just feel like fainting."

"Claudia — " Kristy began.

"What was his name?" Claudia asked, closing her eyes as she tried to think. "Robin? Robert? Roger! That's it. Roger. Roger Casey." She sighed. "He was so cute. I was devastated when he left school because his family moved to Kansas."

"That's all very sad, Claudia," said Kristy sarcastically. "But what on earth does it have to do with what we're talking about?"

"Oh! Right," said Claud a little dreamily. I could tell she was still thinking about those laser-beam eyes.

"Claudia, tell us," I prodded her. I knew she was onto something, but so far I didn't have a clue as to what it might be. "Why are you telling us about this guy?"

"Here's the thing," said Claudia. "I had such a crush on him, and I was so sad when he moved. My only consolation was that when the yearbook came out I'd have a picture of him, to remember him by. But when the yearbook came out, he wasn't in it, because he had left school before pictures were taken."

"So?" asked Kristy. "That's what I was just saying. This girl wouldn't be in the yearbook." She looked confused, and a little irritated.

"Aha!" said Claudia. "But here's the kicker. I'll never forget turning to the page where Roger's picture should have been. It wasn't there. Instead, three pages later, there was a little list of all the people 'not pictured.' "

"So what are you saying?" I asked. "That Roger wasn't the only one?" Now *I* was confused.

"I see!" said Logan, jumping out of his chair. "She's saying that there was a *list*! Of *names*."

"Names of people who left school before the year was out!" Mary Anne exclaimed.

"So all we have to do — " Abby began.

"Is check that year's yearbook!" I finished. "This girl's name will be on the 'not pictured' list! Claudia, you're a genius!"

Claudia smiled. "I am," she admitted. "And I owe it all to a diet based on chocolate and chips." She cracked up. "Come on, what are we waiting for? Let's hit the library!"

We cleaned up our table and headed back

to the yearbooks. We grabbed the one from the year of the dance. Sure enough, there was a short list of names on the last page of the eighth-grade section. "Not pictured," it read, "are Julia Berkman, Elizabeth Connor, Herbert Franks, Susan Hsia, Steven Levy, and Mark Whipple."

"Three boys and three girls," said Mary Anne. "I wonder what happened to them?"

"The question is, which one is the girl we want to know about, and what happened to *her*?" I asked. I stared at the names, as if I could figure out everything if I looked at them hard enough.

"It could be any one of them," said Abby. "How are we going to find out which it is?"

"We'd need to find out why each of them isn't in the yearbook," said Kristy. "Like, did she move, or was she expelled, or what?"

"But how do we find that out?" I moaned. "This is just another dead end." I was bummed out. We had come so far, and now we were stuck.

"Um, no it's not. Not exactly," said Logan, clearing his throat nervously. "I think I know how we can find the information."

"You do?" Kristy asked him. She narrowed her eyes. "How?"

"Well," said Logan, glancing around to see if anyone else was listening, "it's like this."

He waved us closer, and we bent our heads to listen as he whispered. "One time, Alan Gray and I were poking around in the basement — "

"Logan!" Mary Anne hissed. "We're not supposed to go down there!"

"I know," he said. "That's why I'm whispering."

"Oh. Okay, go on."

"Anyway," he continued, after shooting Mary Anne a grin, "we found this dusty old storage room, packed with ancient records." He gave us a significant look, and we looked back blankly. I thought he was talking about old Bee Gees albums.

Logan sighed. "Like, *student* records," he explained, a little impatiently.

"Ohhhh," I said, finally understanding. "Wow! Really?"

"So you mean we might be able to check the records on each of these three girls?" Claudia asked.

"That's exactly what I mean," said Logan.

"But we're not allowed down there," Mary Anne reminded us. "Shouldn't we just ask somebody, like Mr. Kingbridge, or one of the teachers?"

"Are you kidding?" Logan said. "If we did that, we'd never find out any answers. Nobody wants to talk about what happened at that dance. They'd never let us look through the records."

"I'm ready to go," said Abby, standing up. Her eyes were gleaming. "Lead the way, Logan."

He checked his watch. "We don't have time now," he said. "Lunch period's nearly over. How about if we meet here right after school?"

We all agreed that we would, even Mary Anne. And later that day, less than five minutes after the last bell, we were standing outside the library door, ready to do some detective work. I'd told Jessi and Mal to come, too, and they were as excited as the rest of us.

"I've never even been in the basement," said Mal.

"That's because you're a sixth-grader," Logan joked. "You're too young to be initiated into the deepest mysteries of SMS."

"But we can come with you now, can't we?" asked Jessi.

"You bet," said Logan, grinning. He turned to face the rest of us. "Everybody ready?"

"Ready," I replied.

"Definitely ready," said Abby, rubbing her hands together in anticipation. "I want to really get to know my new school!"

"Ready, I guess," said Mary Anne hesitantly.

"I'm better than ready, I'm prepared," said Claud, holding up a bag of M&Ms. "I brought provisions, in case we end up lost down there in the deepest mysteries of SMS."

"Then what are we waiting for?" asked Kristy. "Lead the way, Logan." She had a determined look in her eye, but I had the feeling that even Kristy might be the tiniest bit nervous about what we were going to do.

The fact was, we were all nervous. Even Logan. Even Abby. But we tried to hide it as we followed Logan down the stairs marked "No Entry." The stairwell was dimly lit, and our footsteps echoed as we descended into the ever-darker basement. Finally, at the bottom, Logan pushed open a heavy door and waved us through.

Then the door slammed shut behind us.

"Oh, my Lord!"

"Is it locked?"

"We're trapped!"

Everybody started to panic, but Logan raised his voice above the din. "Quiet, everybody," he said. "It's not locked. I made sure of that. Don't worry, we're fine."

By the time he'd finished talking, we had calmed down — a little. I looked around and saw that we were in a dark hallway with several doors opening off of it. All the doors looked the same, but Logan led us confidently to the third one on the right. He looked uncertain as he tried the knob, but then a grin lit up his face and he pushed the door open. "Here we are," he said.

It was a little lighter inside the room, because two small basement windows, high up in the walls, let in some sun. But it wasn't exactly what you'd call bright. There was just enough light for us to see pile upon pile of cardboard file boxes, covered with layers of dust and festooned with cobwebs.

"Nobody's cleaned in here for a while," joked Kristy.

Abby sneezed three times in a row. "This dust!" she said. She reached into her backpack, pulled out a surgical mask, and put it on. "I should have dode," she said in a stuffed-up voice.

"How do we start?" I asked. "It would take months to look through every box."

"We don't have to," said Logan. "They're pretty well labeled. All we have to do is find the one from that year."

Logan turned out to be right. It wasn't hard to find the box we needed, and, fortunately, the records inside were neatly alphabetized. I had written down the names of the three girls listed in the yearbook, and it didn't take long to pull out their records. I passed out the files, and everybody started to page through them.

Then I riffled quickly through the box and grabbed one more file, just out of curiosity.

"I have Julia Berkman's file," Kristy reported, "and it says here that she transferred in the following March, to a school for the performing arts."

"Lucky!" Jessi murmured.

"She's not the one we're looking for," said Claudia. "Keep checking."

"Here's Susan Hsia's file," Mary Anne said. "It seems as if her family moved, and I'm trying to figure out when. Oh, here it is. They moved to Sioux Falls — is that in Iowa? — in December."

"It's id South Dakota," said Abby, still sniffing. "But I dod't think we deed to go out there to track dowd Susad. She's dot our girl, if she left school in Decebber."

Mal was looking through the third file. As I waited, I opened the file I'd grabbed. It was Michael Rothman's. I scanned it quickly and discovered that he *was* on the football team, and that he had been an average student. There was nothing else very interesting, except for one mention, by a counselor, about "Michael's extreme fear of heights." Hmmm.

"Hold on, hold on!" shouted Mal suddenly, interrupting my thoughts. "This is it! I'm *positive!*"

We clustered around to look over her shoulder. "It's Elizabeth Connor," breathed Claudia.

"All it says is that she left school in early November," Mal said. "No further explanation."

"That's our girl," I said. "It has to be her."

"And check it out!" exclaimed Jessi. "Where it gives her address? That's the Johanssens' house, on Kimball Street."

"Wow!" said Mary Anne. "That's a coincidence. And I have a sitting job there tonight."

"Too bad Elizabeth doesn't still live there," I said. "I'd love to interview her."

Suddenly, Mary Anne and I looked at each other, and I could tell we'd both had the same great idea.

CHAPTER 12

Tuesday

Thank goodness for Ghostbusters! The kids were so involved in looking for ectoplasm that they never even noticed that we were hunting our own spirit — the spirit of Liz Connor's past.

Just a few hours after the adventure in the SMS basement, I stood on the Johanssens' front porch, waiting for Mary Anne to answer the door. With me were Matt and Haley Braddock. I was sitting for them that night, and they'd been enthusiastic when, after I'd given them an early dinner, I'd suggested a visit to Charlotte's house. (The parents of all three kids had already okayed the idea.) At nine, Haley is a year older than Charlotte, while Matt is a year younger, but the kids are friends. That's why the plan Mary Anne and I had devised seemed so perfect. We were hoping that if the kids kept each other busy, the two of us would have some time to explore the Johanssens' house, in search of any traces of Elizabeth Connor that still might exist.

It was hard to imagine finding anything new in the Johanssens' house, which is almost as familiar to me as my own. I've spent a lot of time there, since Charlotte is one of my favorite kids to sit for. Actually, she's more than that. She's like a younger sister to me. As only children, we have a special kind of bond.

Also, besides sitting for Charlotte, I've done some sitting for her family's house. Not too long ago, I spent two weeks house-sitting there while the family took a trip to France. I cared for their dog Carrot and kept an eye on the house. I thought it was going to be an easy job, but it turned out to be, well, challenging. The problem was, somebody *else* was spending time in the Johanssens' house during those two weeks — and I had had to find out who it was. Believe me, it wasn't an easy mystery to solve, but fortunately, everything turned out all right.

Anyway, as I was saying, the Johanssens' house is very familiar to me. Everything from the dried-flower wreath on the front door to the blue-tiled floor in the neat kitchen seems welcoming and homelike.

I didn't stand on the porch for long. Mary Anne, Charlotte, and Carrot answered the door together, and they were excited. Mary Anne was happy to see me, Charlotte was thrilled to have Matt and Haley for company on a school night, and Carrot was just generally keyed up. He's a schnauzer: a gray dog, with bushy eyebrows, a stubby tail, and a muscular body. I always think Carrot moves as if he has springs inside, and that night was no exception.

"Okay, Carrot, okay," I said, trying to calm him down. "Good dog." (I'm not a huge pet lover, but I am fond of Carrot.) "Hi, Mary Anne. Hi, Charlotte. How are you two?"

"We're fine," said Charlotte, giving me a quick hug. Then she turned to greet Haley and

Matt. "Hey, you guys," she said. "What do you want to do tonight?"

Haley signed to Matt, translating. Matt is deaf, and communicates with American Sign Language. Everyone in the BSC has learned to sign at least a little bit, though Jessi's the only one of us who is really any good. For the most part, we rely on Haley when we need to communicate anything complicated to Matt.

Matt didn't even wait for Haley to finish. He must have figured out what Charlotte had said without needing any translation. He signed back rapidly, and Haley nodded enthusiastically. She turned to Charlotte. "Want to play Ghostbusters?" she asked.

"Definitely!" said Charlotte. "After school today I worked on my collection unit. It's cool. I also made a ghost detector. We can ghostbust the whole house. Want to come upstairs? I'll show you my stuff."

Two seconds later, the kids had thundered up the stairs, and Mary Anne and I were alone in the living room. "That was easy," I said. "I was a little worried about how we were going to keep them occupied while we searched the house."

"We should have known," said Mary Anne, laughing. "Ghostbuster fever strikes again!"

"It's perfect for us, too," I said. "The kids

will want to check out the whole house, and we can just follow them from room to room, doing our own detective work. Only we won't be looking for ghosts — unless Elizabeth Connor happens to be one." I thought for a second. "You know, as a matter of fact, we don't know if she's still alive or not. She really might be a ghost."

"Stop it," said Mary Anne, grinning as she covered her ears. "I don't even want to think about that possibility."

"I guess if she is a ghost," I mused, "the kids will take care of her. She'll end up in one of those collection units."

"Which would be right where she belongs," said Mary Anne.

"Where who belongs?" asked Haley, who had just come back downstairs, along with Charlotte and Matt.

"Oh, nobody," I said quickly. "Are you guys all set for ghostbusting?"

"Can't you tell?" asked Charlotte. She stood in front of us and twirled around so we could see the equipment that festooned her body. She wore a flashlight in a holster attached to a belt and a homemade contraption (it looked a lot like the one Arnold had made) in a backpack-style sling. She had on what must have been her mother's gardening gloves, which came up to her elbows, and her head was protected by a bike helmet.

Matt and Haley were also suited up. Matt was wearing a colander on his head, while Haley wore a metal pot. Matt had on a pair of leather work gloves, and Haley wore two oven mitts. (The kids had obviously made a trip to the kitchen.) Both of them carried complicated-looking devices made from shoeboxes.

"One, and two, and three," Haley said, raising her arms as if conducting an orchestra. She and Charlotte sang in unison while Matt signed emphatically, three verses and two choruses of the *Ghostbusters* song, ending with a shouted "Who you gonna call? *GHOSTBUSTERS!*"

Mary Anne and I applauded loudly. Then we looked at each other solemnly. "I guess they're ready," I said.

"Sure looks like it," Mary Anne agreed. "Okay, kids, where are you going to start?"

Haley rolled her eyes, as if the question were a ridiculous one. "In the attic, of course," she replied. "That's the most likely spot for ghosts. Then we'll work our way down through the house, checking in every closet and under every bed."

"If we find any slime, I'm all ready to take a sample," said Charlotte.

Matt signed something quickly, and Haley

translated, "And Matt says he's all set to take readings."

"Let's go, then," I said, leading the way toward the attic stairs. I gave Mary Anne a Look over the kids' heads, one that said, "Don't forget, we're searching for signs of Elizabeth Connor." She nodded, and I knew she'd understood.

Up in the attic, a single bare bulb cast a little light in the center of the room, but the rest of the attic was in shadow. The kids went wild. They poked into every corner, shouting for any hidden ghosts to come out and face their fate. Charlotte aimed her flashlight into every nook and cranny, while Matt followed her with a serious look on his face and the ghost detector at the ready. Haley stood by, waiting to hear that somebody had found a ghost so she could collect it.

Meanwhile, Mary Anne and I quickly searched the attic. I was checking for any boxes or trunks that might have been left behind by previous occupants, while Mary Anne peered into the spaces between the eaves, looking for, as she told me in a whisper, "letters or notes or anything Elizabeth might have left."

Unfortunately, the Johanssens' attic is one of the neatest, tidiest attics I've ever seen. We didn't find a thing.

Apparently, the kids didn't either. "I think we can declare this area free of ghosts," said Haley, after they'd toured the entire attic. "Do you agree, Dr. Braddock?" She was looking at Matt, and she signed as she spoke. Matt nodded vehemently. "How about you, Doctor Johanssen?" she asked Charlotte.

"The readings show no signs of ghosts," agreed Charlotte. "And there's no sign of any slime. I think we can move on."

Charlotte led the way down the stairs, and her two friends trooped behind her as she headed into her bedroom. "I've checked this area before," she said, "but you can't be too careful." Her "colleagues" agreed. Again, the kids went over every square inch of the room.

So did Mary Anne and I. Only we weren't looking for ghosts. We were looking for — what? I wasn't even sure. What kind of signs might Elizabeth have left behind? I puzzled over that problem as I poked around near Charlotte's bookcase.

"Psst!" I heard Mary Anne hiss, and I turned to see her waving me over to Charlotte's closet door. "Check it out!" she said, pointing to the doorframe. Her eyes were bright and her cheeks were pink. Obviously she'd found something very interesting.

"Check what out?" I asked.

"The *doorframe*!" she said.

"What about it?" I asked. I gave it a quick look, but didn't see anything out of the ordinary.

"Look closer," she said. "See the marks?"

I bent to examine the wood more closely. Just then, somebody tapped me on the shoulder, and I jumped. But it was only Charlotte. "We're moving on to the next room," she said. "Meet you there?"

"Sure," I said. "Find any ghosts in here?"

She shook her head. "Nothing so far. But we will. I'm sure of it." She headed off, followed by Matt and Haley.

I turned back to the doorframe and inspected it carefully. Then I saw what Mary Anne had been talking about. "Awesome," I breathed. "So she really *did* live here." There, on the wood, covered lightly with one coat of white paint, were height markings for "Elizabeth." One for each year, from the time she was only tall enough to reach my belly button to the time she was just about the same height as Mary Anne is now.

"We're on the right track, anyway," said Mary Anne, "even if this doesn't tell us much about her."

"Let's keep looking," I said. "You never know what we might find."

After that, we trailed the kids through the house, always staying about one room behind as they checked for ghosts and we sought signs of Elizabeth Connor. As far as I could tell from what I overheard the kids saying, they weren't finding much. Neither were we.

The last place we all checked was the basement, and the kids swept through it quickly. Finally, Charlotte gave up. "I guess I've scared all the ghosts out of this house already," she told Mary Anne. "Can we go to the kitchen and have some cookies? Mom said I could have two for dessert."

"Sure," said Mary Anne. "Go on up. We'll be there in a second."

The kids thundered up the stairs, leaving Mary Anne and me alone in the dimly lit basement. "This is our last chance," she said. "Let's look carefully."

Five minutes later, I was ready to give up too. "There's nothing here," I said. "We'd better head upstairs and make sure the kids are all right."

"Hold on, hold on," said Mary Anne, bending to look at a spot on the floor. "What's this?" She brushed away some dirt and looked more closely. I joined her, and saw a place where the cement floor had been patched with a lighter-colored cement. Etched into the patched place were these letters, inside a heart:

"L.C. and Mister?" Mary Anne said, in a puzzled voice.

"No!" I cried. Just then, I felt as if one of those cartoon light bulbs was flashing on over my head. "Liz Connor and Mike Rothman."

CHAPTER **13**

Liz Connor and Mike Rothman. Mike Rothman and Liz Connor. Could it be true? Maybe I was going nuts. After all, I was taking some pretty wild guesses. I had no idea, really, whether or not Elizabeth Connor was known as "Liz." In fact, I knew next to nothing about Elizabeth Connor. Still, I couldn't help thinking that she was the key, and that solving this twenty-eight-year-old mystery would help us figure out what was happening at SMS now. And it sure was a mystery. For example, what about those other initials? Did MR really stand for Mike Rothman? And was that Mike Rothman the same Mike Rothman I knew?

These were the questions chasing each other through my mind on Wednesday afternoon as I stood in the middle of the gym, holding one end of a roll of red crepe paper while Todd walked away from me, unfurling it to its full length. The dance was only two days away, so Todd and I and the rest of the decorations committee were finally starting our real job: decorating the gym.

So far, it was hard to tell whether our theme was going to work. The gym, in broad daylight, is hardly the most romantic spot in the world. The floors are squeaky, there's dust everywhere, and a certain . . . *odor* hangs in the air, reminding you of the thousands of basketball games that must have been played there over the years.

It was hard to imagine the transformation that would have to take place by Friday night. Still, I had high hopes. I'd seen the gym transformed before, for other dances, and it's always amazed me how magical the place can look. Magical and, yes, even romantic.

I let myself daydream a little about Friday night. Robert and I hadn't had much time for dating recently, so I was really looking forward to spending the evening with him. We'd decided to go as Morticia and Gomez Addams, because of the theme of the dance. I knew I would look bewitching in a long black wig and a form-fitting black dress, and I was sure Robert would look handsomer than ever, dressed as the dashing Gomez.

I tried to picture us together, having a terrific time at a terrific dance. We would drink punch and laugh with our friends. We'd dance wildly to the fast songs, and then hold each other close for the slow ones. It would be wonderful — wouldn't it?

I wasn't so sure. I couldn't ignore the fact that something was wrong. I had a bad feeling about this dance. It was almost as if someone had put a curse on it. And I couldn't shake the idea that unless I solved the mystery in time, the dance was going to be a disaster. Even the decorating committee was under the curse. Not only had our stuff been vandalized, but now Grace and Cokie weren't speaking to each other. Grace had found out that Cokie didn't believe in Ted and they'd had a huge fight. As a result, our meetings were a little more tense.

"Stacey! Heads up!" I looked up just in time to see Grace, who was standing on a stepladder, toss me a roll of purple crepe paper. I caught it with my free hand and held onto my end while she fastened the other end to a rafter. Meanwhile, Todd was securing the other end of the red roll to the wall over the main entrance. Rick and Cokie were setting up tables under one of the scoreboards, for punch and cookies. Mr. Rothman walked around, supervising and offering suggestions.

I looked at him out of the corner of my eye, trying not to be caught staring. Was he the Mike Rothman from the yearbook? If so, why hadn't he told us he'd attended SMS way back when? Was he trying to hide something?

"Mr. Rothman, Mr. Rothman!" Todd called. "Can you help me over here?"

"Sure, Todd. What can I do?" I watched as Mr. Rothman walked to where Todd was standing.

"Take this end of the roll," Todd directed, handing Mr. Rothman a new roll of red paper, "and attach it up there." He pointed to a spot on the other side of the gym. Grace had left the ladder set up beneath it. "I'll hold this end."

"Um, okay," said Mr. Rothman. He started to walk toward the ladder, and then he stopped. "Tell you what, Todd," he said. "How about if *you* attach it?"

"Sure, no problem," said Todd. "You stand right here, then." Todd walked away from Mr. Rothman, unrolling the paper as he went. I looked back at Mr. Rothman just in time to see him wipe his brow. But it wasn't hot in the gym, not at all. In fact, it was downright chilly. Why was Mr. Rothman sweating?

I kept an eye on Mr. Rothman as he watched Todd climb the ladder, and suddenly, everything clicked into place. I saw the look on Mr. Rothman's face, and I knew why he hadn't wanted to climb that ladder. It was because he was afraid — make that terrified — of heights.

Just like the Mike Rothman whose file I'd seen in the basement.

That's when I knew for sure that this Mike Rothman was the very same Mike Rothman who had been in the yearbook. And then and there, I decided it was time to find out more about what Mike Rothman knew.

I walked over to him. My mind was racing, but I couldn't figure out a clever way to bring up the subject. "Hi, Mr. Rothman."

"Hello, Stacey," he answered, smiling at me. "What's on your mind?"

"Liz Connor," I said, without thinking. "Liz Connor is on my mind."

Mr. Rothman turned pale. For a second, I thought he was going to pass out. He let go of the crepe paper he was holding. "Liz Connor?" he said. "How do you know about Liz?"

That's when I knew I had guessed right. He didn't try to deny anything, or make up lies about who he was. I was on my way to learning the truth. I took a deep breath, and explained what I knew so far. It didn't take long, since I didn't know much. I told him how I'd figured out his past, and then how I'd learned that a girl had been involved in that tragic dance long ago, and how my friends and I had figured out who the girl must be. (I sort of fudged the part about our explorations in the basement.) Then I told him about finding his

124

initials in the heart at Charlotte's house, and I saw him close his eyes as if he were in pain.

"That's it," I concluded. "That's all I know. Now I need you to fill in the blanks."

He sighed. "I suppose it's time," he said. "This story has been haunting me for twenty-eight years. Let's go sit down, and I'll tell you all about it." He led me to a spot in the bleachers, away from everyone else. We sat together, and then he was quiet for a long time. I was about to ask him some questions, but finally he began to speak.

"I was on the football team," he said, in a faraway voice.

I pictured him in a helmet and uniform. That *had* been him in the yearbook.

"I was one of the most popular kids in school," Mr. Rothman continued. "I was good-looking, I was fun to be with, and I was an excellent athlete." He looked at me. "I don't mean to sound stuck up, but it's true. That's just the way it was." He smiled a bittersweet smile. "The girls were crazy about me, but I didn't take advantage of that, the way some guys on the team did. My mother brought me up to be a gentleman, and that's what I was. I dated, sure, but there was nobody special. And I treated *all* the girls with respect."

"What about Liz?" I asked. When was he going to answer my question?

"Liz," he said with a sigh. "Liz Connor was a shy girl. Quiet. Not giggly like the other girls. She wasn't popular. In fact, when she was noticed at all, it was only because somebody was making fun of her."

"But you noticed her," I prompted him.

"I was nice to her," he said. "I was nice to everybody. But since nobody else was nice to Liz, I guess it meant a lot to her. She developed a big crush on me — at least, according to the other kids. She didn't know they knew. She thought her crush was a secret. But it wasn't. It was a big joke to everybody."

"Oops," I said.

"It gets worse. See, when my friends on the football team heard that there was going to be a costume dance on the night before Halloween that year, they came up with a plan. They thought it would be hilarious if I asked Liz to the dance. They cornered me, and dared me to do it." He paused. "And then, just to up the ante, they bet me ten dollars that I wouldn't last the whole evening with her."

"But you refused, right?" I asked.

He shook his head sadly. "I wish I had. But being popular was so important to me. I knew it was wrong, but I did it anyway. I figured I'd ask her out, and tell her later about the bet. Maybe I'd even split the money with her.

I didn't realize how serious she was about me. I thought she'd think the whole thing was silly, just like I did."

"And?" I asked.

"I asked her to the dance, at school, in front of a bunch of my friends. She didn't have a clue that I wasn't being sincere. She was thrilled to be invited."

"Poor Liz," I said. I could just imagine how she felt. How could she know that was a joke?

"By the time the dance rolled around, I was feeling so guilty I could hardly stand it," Mr. Rothman continued. "I went to Liz's house to pick her up, and she came downstairs in this ridiculous, elaborate, babyish fairy princess costume. She looked pretty, but she looked about nine years old. I felt even worse when I saw her, because I knew the other kids were going to laugh at her costume. I realized then that there was no way I could tell her about the bet. I was just going to have to stick it out and hope for the best."

I winced. "Didn't she know her costume was silly?"

He shook his head. "I'm sure she didn't. You should have seen her when we walked into the gym. Everybody was snickering and whispering, but she didn't notice a thing. She just took my arm and smiled up at me, and I knew she was proud to be my date. I felt like the lowest of the low. I knew exactly what was going on, but Liz was oblivious. One girl, sort of a friend of hers, walked by and hissed into my ear 'How dare you?' It was awful."

"Did you stick it out?" I asked. "Did you win the ten dollars?" I knew my tone was nasty, but I felt angry at that Mike Rothman of so long ago.

"I'm coming to that," he answered. "Once the music started, things were a little better. After all, at least we could dance. And boy, did we dance! I didn't want Liz to spend a second alone, since somebody might spill the beans. I couldn't bring her over to be with my friends. And I sure didn't want to stand around and talk. So we danced and danced, to every single song." He smiled. "Liz was having a great time, and you know what? I could have been, too. If only I'd been honest with her, and with myself. But instead, I was caught in the biggest lie of my life."

"So how did it turn out?" I asked.

"The band announced that it was almost time for the 'last dance.' Liz ran off to the powder room, and I talked to my friends. When she came back, I joined her right away, but she'd seen me with them, and she'd seen how uncomfortable I'd looked. She asked me what was wrong, but I didn't answer. Then the band started playing 'Will You Still Love Me Tomorrow?' "

I gasped, remembering the letters in dripping red paint.

Mr. Rothman barely noticed. He was deeply involved in his story. "When I didn't take Liz into my arms for the dance, she asked me again what was wrong. I shook my head. Then I said, 'I can't do this.' I looked around and saw that nobody else was dancing either. They were all watching us. Liz saw it, too. 'I just can't do it,' I said again, and I broke away from her. As I walked away, I took a ten-dollar bill from my pocket and threw it onto the floor, just to show my friends how little the money meant to me."

"But Liz — " I began.

"The money landed at her feet," he said. "She was totally humiliated, standing there alone in the middle of the dance floor. A few kids started to laugh. Liz looked around at the crowd one more time, and from what I heard later, this time she looked angry. Then she walked out the door and slammed it behind her. A couple of minutes later, the power went off in the gym."

"And then?"

"Then the fire alarm went off — because

somebody pulled it — and that's when everybody stampeded. Three hundred kids tried to leave the gym, all at the same time. It must have been a madhouse."

"And Mr. Brown died," I said.

Mr. Rothman nodded. "Of a heart attack," he said. "There's never been another Mischief Night masquerade."

"What about Liz?" I asked.

"She never came back to school," he answered. "Her family moved away, and nobody's heard of her since."

Both of us were quiet for a few seconds. Then Mr. Rothman gave me a tired smile. "This is why I wanted to work on your dance," he said. "Just to make sure everything goes smoothly this time."

"But it hasn't," I said.

"No," he admitted. "But we can't let a few pranksters ruin things for us, can we?"

Did Mr. Rothman really believe that "pranksters" were responsible for trying to ruin our dance? He might have — until he and I walked into the gym together early the next morning, to do a final check on the decorations. What we saw chilled me to the bone.

There, hanging by a noose from one of the basketball hoops, was a dummy. A dummy dressed in a pink, frothy, fairy princess costume.

Mr. Rothman turned white. Then he said three of the scariest words I've ever heard: "Liz is back."

CHAPTER 14

"Ooh, look," said Mary Anne. "It's all lit up. I can't wait to go in."

My friends and I stood in the parking lot, looking up at the school. It was Mischief Night, and we were about to enter the dance. Yellow light spilled out of the school's big windows, and I could hear faint music as the band warmed up. I couldn't wait, either. But I was more than a little afraid. I still had a strong feeling that something was going to go wrong — very wrong — at the dance. Our detective work had turned up all the pieces of the puzzle, but somehow I couldn't fit them together. I shivered, and thought again about the dummy Mr. Rothman and I had seen.

He and I had talked it over. Could Liz Connor really be back in Stoneybrook? And if so, what was she after? Did she have revenge on her mind? We checked the local phone directories to see if her name was listed, but it wasn't. We considered speaking to Mr. Kingbridge, or even to the police, but then we realized how ridiculous our story sounded. It was like something out of a bad horror movie. Finally, we couldn't think of anything else to do. The decorations were ready. Everybody's costumes were planned. Every ticket was sold. The dance was on.

I had told my friends everything I'd learned, and they were primed to keep an eye open for Liz Connor, for Mr. Wetzler, for the Mischief Knights, for anything that might happen at the dance, including an appearance by the ghost of Mr. Brown. But none of the other BSC members was as worried as I was about the outcome of the dance. How could they be? None of them had seen that awful dummy hanging in the gym, and none of them had heard the fear in Mr. Rothman's voice.

As I dressed that night, and then again as I stood in the parking lot with the other members of the BSC, I tried to forget my fears and concentrate on how much fun the dance might turn out to be. Maybe the Mischief Knights *were* responsible for all the pranks, and maybe the dance would go smoothly.

Maybe.

Or maybe not.

Either way, there was nothing else I could do. I took a deep breath and looked around at my friends. They all wore masks to hide their identities, but of course I knew who they were. Their costumes were terrific.

Mary Anne wore a childish dress (one of the ones left over from when her father was so strict) with a pinafore over it. She wore a pigtail wig and she carried a picnic basket. She made a perfect Dorothy. The best part was that Logan had decided to dress as the Scarecrow, and together the two of them looked as if they'd just stepped out of Oz.

Originally Mal had planned to dress as a cowgirl and Jessi was going to be a ballerina. But they had decided to switch costumes, just for fun. Jessi wore a fringed leather skirt and jacket, cowboy boots, and a ten-gallon hat. She looked awesome. And Mal, wearing an old Swan Lake costume of Jessi's, looked great, too.

Abby had gone ahead with her plan to dress as Lucy Ricardo. Her mom had helped her color her hair bright red with temporary dye. She wore an old-fashioned dress like the ones Lucy wore on her show, and her mouth was outlined in red lipstick that was almost as bright as her hair.

Kristy looked dashing as Amelia Earhart. She wore a leather jacket (her brother's), high boots, a long white silk scarf, and an old-fashioned helmet and goggles (Watson had found them for her). And Claudia looked, well, delicious as a giant Twinkie. She'd made the costume herself, using cardboard and poster paints.

How could the evening not be fun if I was spending it with such a great group? I smiled over at Robert, who made a devastating Gomez Addams in his dark suit. "Shall we go in, my dear?" he asked, stroking his glued-on mustache.

"*Oui, oui,*" I said with a smile.

"Tish! That French!" he cried. He grabbed my arm and started to kiss his way up it. I giggled. Suddenly I was in the mood to have fun. "Let's go," I said to my friends. We headed into the school, handed over our tickets, and entered the gym.

"Awesome!" breathed Mal, taking it all in.

"You guys did a fantastic job!" Kristy exclaimed. "I've never seen this place look so cool."

"Those portraits are perfect, Claud," said Logan. "They add just the right creepy touch."

The gym did look pretty amazing. The red lights created a mood and helped hide such things as the basketball hoops. Every detail our committee had added came together to give the illusion of a creaky old mansion filled

filled with spiderwebs, weird furniture, and surprises around every corner. As Morticia Addams, I felt right at home.

The band was already playing, and plenty of people were on the dance floor. I just stood there for a while, letting my eyes become used to the darkness as I scoped out the costumes people were wearing.

"Look, there's Cokie," said Kristy, pointing to a girl in an old-fashioned bonnet and pinafore. She carried a hooked staff with ribbons tied around it. "Little Bo Peep, my eye," snorted Kristy. "That's a laugh. She should be dressed as the Wicked Witch of the West."

I couldn't help laughing, too.

"There's Grace," said Claudia. "She looks cute. Who's her date? What a hunk!"

Sure enough, there was Grace (dressed as Snow White), dancing with an incredibly cute guy who was dressed as Prince Charming. I saw them dance right by Cokie, but Grace didn't even glance at her former best friend.

"So Ted really does exist," I murmured to myself. I was happy for Grace, and it was a relief to be absolutely certain that I'd been wrong to suspect her of the vandalism.

I saw Todd and Rick standing by the refreshments table, next to the steaming punch bowl. Todd had come as Fred Flintstone, and

Rick was Barney Rubble. Their costumes were a riot.

It was so much fun to see everyone dressed up that I almost forgot my fears about the evening. But then Mr. Rothman danced by, dressed as a football player (including helmet and shoulder pads). He gave me a look over his date's shoulder, and I knew *he* hadn't forgotten. Then he and his date (a substitute home ec teacher named Ms. Bryan, who was dressed as a vampire, in a long, black cloak with a hood) whirled away, leaving me with a queasy feeling.

Liz Connor might be somewhere in that crowd, and if she was, she could be ready to make trouble. Or the troublemaker might be Mr. Wetzler, or the Mischief Knights. Or — gulp — the ghost of Mr. Brown. And there wasn't just a middle school dance at stake. This was serious business. If one of those people pulled a prank and the crowd panicked, people could be hurt or even killed.

It had happened before.

I was lost in thought, but Robert brought me back to reality by asking me to dance. I hadn't told him anything about my fears, since I wanted this night to be fun. I just smiled at him and followed him onto the dance floor. Robert is an excellent dancer. I think it's because he's a good athlete and knows how to move his body without feeling self-conscious. We danced to three fast songs until I was out of breath, and then settled into a slow one. I rested my head on Robert's shoulder and relaxed. For a few sweet moments, I forgot everything but the feeling of Robert's arms around me.

Then I felt his arms tighten. "Whoa!" he said. "Check it out!"

I lifted my head and looked around. "What?" I asked.

"That guy's costume is great," he said, nodding toward a figure looming nearby.

I looked closer and realized it was Cary Retlin, dancing with Sabrina Bouvier, who was dressed as Cleopatra. Cary's face barely showed through a peephole in the huge papier-mâché horse head he wore. "A horse?" I asked.

"I think he's supposed to be a chess piece," said Robert. "You know, a what's-it-called?"

"A *knight*!" I said, gasping. "That's Cary Retlin, and he's supposed to be a knight." Suddenly, it all became clear. The mischief that had gone on during recent weeks had started *after* Cary moved to Stoneybrook and came to SMS. Cary Retlin was the leader of the Mischief Knights! He had to be.

Then I remembered something else. I remember how I'd laughed at him his first day in my English class when he fell off his chair. Did he resent me for that? Maybe he did, and maybe he knew I was on the decorations committee for the dance. If so, he had a motive for sabotaging our hard work.

"Robert," I whispered. "Let's switch partners with them. I want to talk to Cary."

"Sure," Robert said. "I always wanted to dance with Cleopatra." He tapped Cary on the shoulder. "Mind if I cut in?" he asked, and before Cary could answer, Robert had taken his place with Sabrina, leaving Cary standing there alone. I held out my arms, and soon we were dancing together. The band shifted into a faster song.

"I know your secret," I whispered to him.

He didn't answer. He just spun me around the dance floor. He was a pretty good dancer.

"I know you're a Mischief Knight," I said, after we'd spun past the stage where the band was playing.

"Do you?" he asked. I couldn't see his face, but I had a feeling he was smiling.

"You're the one who thought up all those pranks," I said. "Aren't you?"

"I don't know," he said teasingly. "Am I?"

It was infuriating. "You are!" I cried.

"Maybe I am and maybe I'm not. Either

way, you have no way of proving anything."

He was right. I had a feeling that SMS, and the BSC, hadn't heard the last of the Mischief Knights.

Robert cut back in on Cary and me before I had a chance to ask any more questions, such as whether or not the Mischief Knights were responsible for vandalizing our dance decorations. It was probably just as well, because he never would have given me a straight answer anyway.

Robert noticed that I was agitated, but when he asked me what was the matter, I told him I was okay. I was, too. Or at least, that's what I told myself. Robert and I danced to every song for a long time after that, which was fine with me. I didn't want to talk, and I didn't want to think. All I wanted was to have a good time and to end the dance without anyone getting hurt.

The evening flew by in a blur. I know my friends were having fun, because every so often I'd see one of them dance by, smiling. Even Mr. Rothman was having fun, from what I could tell. He and Ms. Bryan in her long black cloak were dancing up a storm.

Finally, the band announced that they were going to take a short break, and that when they came back they'd play for the last dance of the night, when everyone would take off

140

their masks and "reveal their identities." That was kind of silly, since everybody already knew who everybody else was, but it would still be fun. I headed for the girls' room to make sure my makeup hadn't melted underneath my mask.

When I walked in, I saw Ms. Bryan standing near the towel dispenser, hugging herself. All she was wearing was a camisole and leggings, and she looked cold — and upset.

"Are you okay?" I asked.

"Oh, I'm fine," she said. "It's just that somebody spilled onion dip all over my cloak, and then followed me here. When I took it off to clean it, they grabbed it and ran off. Now I'm stuck in here. I can't go back out there dressed like this."

I stared at her. "Somebody stole your cloak?" I said slowly.

Just then, I heard the music start up in the gym. The last dance was beginning. Something clicked in my mind. All the pieces of the puzzle flew into place. "Oh, no!" I cried.

I dashed into the gym and stopped short when I saw Mr. Rothman dancing with a woman in a long, black cloak! I ran toward them, without even thinking about what I was going to do or say, but before I could reach them the bandleader announced that it was time for "the unmasking."

"Would everybody please reveal your identity when I count to three," he said. The drummer began a drumroll, and the lights went out. The idea was that when the lights came back on, everybody would be revealed for who they really were. I knew it was planned. This was not a blackout. But all the same, it was frightening — especially when somebody screamed.

The lights flickered on as suddenly as they'd gone off, and I looked over at the spot where I'd seen Mr. Rothman. He was still there, only now he was as white as a sheet. Standing in front of him was a woman wearing a tattered and torn pink fairy princess costume. A black cloak lay at her feet.

Michael Rothman stared at Liz Connor, and she stared back at him with a wild gleam in her eyes. She smiled slowly. Even from where I was standing, it was obvious that Liz Connor was very, very crazy.

CHAPTER 15

"So then what happened?" Shannon leaned forward eagerly.

It was Monday afternoon, and, while we were supposedly having a BSC meeting in Claud's room, we were actually rehashing the events of the weekend. And, naturally, the first thing we did was to fill Shannon in on everything that had happened at the dance, since she was the only BSC member who hadn't been there. She had come to our meeting just to hear about it. I don't know how she made sense of any of it, since we were all talking at once, but at any rate we had told the story up until the point when the lights came back on and Liz Connor was standing in front of Mr. Rothman, dressed in her tattered fairy princess costume.

"It was awesome," said Claudia. "Everybody just stopped what they were doing and stared at them." She shook her head and popped three red Peanut M&Ms into her mouth.

"It was so creepy," said Jessi, with a shudder.

"Majorly creepy," agreed Kristy. "That woman was out of her gourd. It was, like, what's she going to do next?"

"Even the people who didn't know anything about the story were freaked out," said Mal. "Especially when she started laughing."

"She started laughing?" asked Shannon. "You mean, like someone-told-a-joke laughing?"

"No," Abby said. "Like crazed-hyena-in-the-middle-of-the-night laughing."

"She was hysterical," explained Kristy. "Completely and totally hysterical."

"So what did that teacher — Mr. Rothman — do?" asked Shannon.

"He just said, 'Let's go, Liz,' and he led her out of the gym," I replied.

"I thought he was very sweet with her," said Mary Anne.

"Well, he blames himself," I explained. "But it's not really *all* his fault. From what I heard afterward, it sounds as if she were unbalanced to start with, and she'd been slowly becoming more and more disturbed over the years. She was completely obsessed with what had happened to her at that dance twenty-eight years ago. In fact, she's spent a lot of time in mental hospitals since then. That's where she went when she moved away from Stoneybrook."

"Wow," Shannon breathed. "What a story." She helped herself to a handful of M&Ms. "So was she the one who tried to ruin your dance?"

"Oh, didn't we tell you?" Abby asked. "She confessed to everything as Mr. Rothman was leading her out of the gym. She just kept babbling about all the things she'd done. Apparently she had flipped out when she discovered that SMS was planning another Mischief Night masquerade. She did her best to make sure the dance wouldn't happen, especially after she found out that Mr. Rothman had returned to SMS to teach."

"She was responsible for the lights going out in the auditorium that day," Kristy began, ticking things off on her fingers, "and for breaking those light bulbs, and cutting up the streamers — "

"And let's not forget that she ruined my posters," Claudia added, "and painted things on the gym walls."

"I know I'll never forget that dummy she hung from the basketball hoop," I said, shivering. "Talk about creepy!"

"So where is she now?" asked Shannon.

"Back in a hospital," Kristy said. "At least,

that's what today's paper said. I hope someone there can help her."

"I just hope she never turns up at SMS
again," said Mary Anne.

"So does Mr. Rothman," I added. "I saw
him today in the hall, and he *still* looked ghost-
white."

"Well, that might have been because of what
the Mischief Knights did," said Kristy, leaning
back in the director's chair. She grinned.

"Mischief Knights?" I asked. "I didn't know
they were still causing trouble. What happened?" I couldn't believe I hadn't heard
about it.

"They were pulling pranks all day," said
Claudia. "It was as if they wanted everybody
to know they were still active. They left their
signature every time, too."

"Right," said Mary Anne. "Like, they piled
candy corn in one of the trophy bowls in the
display case, and left a note signed MK."

"And they put a Frankenstein mask in some
girl's locker," added Claudia. "You should
have heard her scream when she opened it!"

"What did they do to Mr. Rothman?" I
asked.

"It was silly, really," said Kristy. "They just
stuck one of those pink 'While You Were Out'
messages on his desk, with a note saying that
Liz Connor had called."

"Hmmm. Not so funny, if you'd been through what he'd been through," I said.

"I guess," Kristy agreed. "But basically harmless. I think it's kind of fun having the Mischief Knights around. If Cary Retlin *is* involved, I hope his family doesn't move anytime soon. SMS can use a little lightening up, and I think the Mischief Knights are just the guys to do it."

"As long as the BSC doesn't end up on their bad side," I mused. "I have a feeling that might be dangerous."

"By the way, speaking of candy corn," said Claudia, "wasn't Halloween a gas?"

It had been fun. We had organized a group of sitters and kids, since several parents had called to ask us to take their kids trick-or-treating. Mary Anne, Claudia, Jessi, Mal, and I had taken a big group of kids around our neighborhood. (Kristy and Shannon took their younger brothers and sisters trick-or-treating in their neighborhood, with Abby's help.) Our group included all the Pike kids, plus Becca Ramsey, Charlotte, the Arnold twins, Matt and Haley Braddock, and a few other regular BSC clients.

We sitters wore our costumes from the night before. (Claudia's giant Twinkie costume was the kids' favorite, naturally.) But the hilarious thing was that each and every kid in our group was dressed as — guess what — a Ghostbuster! We had a small army of Ghostbusters, and all of them were outfitted with ray guns and collection units and detectors and ghostbusting tools of every description. Those kids ghostbusted every house within a ten-block radius. They came away with their collection units empty, but their treat bags full to bursting with Halloween candy.

"I hope that's it for Ghostbusters," said Jessi. "If I hear that song one more time, I might throw up!"

"I think Ghostbusters fever might be winding down," Mary Anne said. "I actually heard Carolyn tell Haley that she almost wished she'd dressed as a fairy tale character instead. That was after she saw Grace Blume walk by dressed as Snow White. Grace was out with her little cousins."

"Grace Blume!" I said, frowning. "Don't mention that name in front of me."

"Why not?" asked Mary Anne. "She's okay, as long as you keep her away from Cokie."

"That's it," I replied. "She and Cokie are like this again." I held up two fingers, crossed. "Cokie apologized for not trusting her, and Grace forgave her. And as soon as they started hanging out together again, they were up to their old tricks."

"What did they do?" asked Kristy.

"You won't believe this," said Claudia. I'd already told her about it, and she was furious.

"Well, you know that new art teacher, the one everybody likes so much? Ms. Dwyer?" I said. "She loved the decorations for the dance, and thought they were 'super-creative.' She wanted to know who had come up with the idea for them, because she has a special project that she needs help with."

"That's great!" said Kristy. "So you'll be working with her."

I shook my head. "Not me," I said. "Cokie. She took full credit for the decorations."

"But she hated every idea the committee came up with," said Mal.

"Yup," I said. "But Ms. Dwyer doesn't know that. And Cokie convinced Grace to back her up on her lie. Grace supported everything Cokie said."

"Unbelievable. You really can't trust either one of them, can you?" asked Kristy.

"It's too bad," said Mary Anne. "I thought Grace was going to turn out okay. But I guess Cokie's influence is too strong."

"You know?" I said. "In a way, I really don't mind. Having Cokie and Grace plot against the BSC is just like old times. I mean, it's normal for us. And after all we've been through over the past couple of weeks, I'm happy things are back to normal again."

Ann M. Martin

About the Author

ANN MATTHEWS MARTIN was born on August 12, 1955. She grew up in Princeton, NJ, with her parents and her younger sister, Jane.

Although Ann used to be a teacher and then an editor of children's books, she's now a full-time writer. She gets the ideas for her books from many different places. Some are based on personal experiences. Others are based on childhood memories and feelings. Many are written about contemporary problems or events.

All of Ann's characters, even the members of the Baby-sitters Club, are made up. (So is Stoneybrook.) But many of her characters are based on real people. Sometimes Ann names her characters after people she knows, other times she chooses names she likes.

In addition to the Baby-sitters Club books, Ann Martin has written many other books for children. Her favorite is *Ten Kids, No Pets* because she loves big families and she loves animals. Her favorite Baby-sitters Club book is *Kristy's Big Day*. (By the way, Kristy is her favorite baby-sitter!)

Ann M. Martin now lives in New York. She has two cats, Mouse and Rosie (who's a boy, but that's a long story). Her hobbies are reading, sewing, and needlework — especially making clothes for children.

Look for Mystery #23

ABBY AND THE SECRET SOCIETY

"Do you often do police work on your own time?" I asked. Mary Anne nudged me, and I knew she thought I was asking too many questions. But I was interested.

"Not often," Sergeant Johnson answered, shaking his head. "But this case is different. According to the department, it's closed. But I don't see it that way. This case is very close to my heart, and it won't be closed for me until . . . until . . ."

"Why don't you sit down and tell us about it?" Mary Anne asked in her gentle, "good-listener" voice. She gestured toward a bench. Now *she* was curious.

"When I was a kid, my best friend's name was David Follman," Sergeant Johnson began as soon as we were all settled onto the bench. "When we grew up, I became a cop and he became a reporter. Thirty years ago, he began an investigation into some dirty doings at Dark Woods."

"Like the way they wouldn't let certain people join?" I asked.

"Worse than that," said Sergeant Johnson. "David had heard rumors about a secret society operating out of the club, a group of men who were involved in a blackmail and extortion ring. They were powerful men, made more powerful by joining forces. They acted illegally to force the local townspeople and merchants to do what they wanted them to do: to vote a certain way, for example, or to use a certain contractor to build their new school."

"That's awful!" said Mary Anne.

"David thought so, too," said Sergeant Johnson. "He went undercover to try to infiltrate the society. And I think he was succeeding! But before he could publish his findings, or even share them with me, David died."

"Oh!" Mary Anne gasped. I felt a knot start to grow in my stomach.

Read all the books
about **Stacey**
in the Baby-sitters Club series
by Ann M. Martin

THE BABY-SITTERS CLUB®

Mysteries

by Ann M. Martin

Something mysterious is going on in Stoneybrook, and now you can solve the case with the Baby-sitters! Collect and read these exciting mysteries along with your favorite Baby-sitters Club books!

❏ BAI44084-5	#1	Stacey and the Missing Ring	$3.50
❏ BAI44085-3	#2	Beware, Dawn!	$3.50
❏ BAI44799-8	#3	Mallory and the Ghost Cat	$3.50
❏ BAI44800-5	#4	Kristy and the Missing Child	$3.50
❏ BAI44801-1	#5	Mary Anne and the Secret in the Attic	$3.50
❏ BAI44961-3	#6	The Mystery at Claudia's House	$3.50
❏ BAI44960-5	#7	Dawn and the Disappearing Dogs	$3.50
❏ BAI44959-1	#8	Jessi and the Jewel Thieves	$3.50
❏ BAI44958-3	#9	Kristy and the Haunted Mansion	$3.50
❏ BAI45696-2	#10	Stacey and the Mystery Money	$3.50
❏ BAI47049-3	#11	Claudia and the Mystery at the Museum	$3.50
❏ BAI47050-7	#12	Dawn and the Surfer Ghost	$3.50
❏ BAI47051-1	#13	Mary Anne and the Library Mystery	$3.50
❏ BAI47052-3	#14	Stacey and the Mystery at the Mall	$3.50

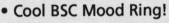
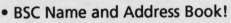
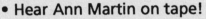

THE BABY-SITTERS CLUB®

by Ann M. Martin

Meet the best friends you'll ever have!

Now THE BABY-SITTERS CLUB®

★ is a Video Club too! ★

What's the scoop with Dawn, Kristy, Mallory, and the other girls?

Be the first to know with G*I*R*L* magazine!

Hey, Baby-sitters Club readers! Now you can be the first on the block to get in on the action of G*I*R*L* It's an exciting new magazine that lets you dig in and read...

★ Upcoming selections from Ann Martin's Baby-sitters Club books
★ Fun articles on handling stress, turning dreams into great careers, making and keeping best friends, and much more
★ Plus, all the latest on new movies, books, music, and sports!

To get in on the scoop, just cut and mail this coupon today. And don't forget to tell all your friends about G*I*R*L* magazine!

A neat offer for you...6 issues for only $15.00.

Sign up today -- this special offer ends July 1, 1996!

❏ **YES!** Please send me G*I*R*L* magazine. I will receive six fun-filled issues for only $15.00. Enclosed is a check (no cash, please) made payable to G*I*R*L* for $15.00.

Just fill in, cut out, and mail this coupon with your payment of $15.00 to: G*I*R*L*, c/o Scholastic Inc., 2931 East McCarty Street, Jefferson City, MO 65101.

Name _____

Address _____

City, State, ZIP _____

9013